MILO SPECK,

ACCIDENTAL AGENT

MILO SPECK,
ACCIDENTAL AGENT

LINDA URBAN
Illustrated by Mariano Epelbaum

HOUGHTON MIFFLIN HARCOURT

BOSTON NEW YORK

www.hmhco.com

The text was set in Dante MT Std.

Library of Congress Cataloging-in-Publication Data is available.

ISBN 978-0-544-41951-3

Manufactured in the United States of America

DOC 10 9 8 7 6 5 4 3 2 1

4500543809

For, and because of, Jack

1

Where Would You Be?

Milo had read about magic before. He knew that kids in stories sometimes found magic in secret drawers or hidden away in attics, and he had always hoped that if he were to find magic, it would appear in the form of a mysterious silver coin or a doorway to an enchanted world. But when magic came to Milo Speck, it came in the form of a sock.

"Figures," said Milo.

Grandmother, who believed that chores built character and kept young boys like Milo out of trouble, had left him a laundry basket full of socks to sort and match in pairs. It was a dreary task, particularly when it came to matching up his father's socks, which were all navy blue with white spots, it seemed—though Grandmother insisted that some of the spots were actually dots and that both the spots and the dots were not all white, but light blue or pale pink or ivory or gray or beige, and should Milo become careless and match a blue-spot sock with a pink-dot sock, his father might not notice the error and might wear the mismatched pair to his job at Tuckerman Fencing and Mr. Tuckerman's assistant—who noticed everything—would surely think his father a dolt and have him sacked, and then where would they be?

Milo wished he knew. He hoped they would be someplace marvelous, like in the books he and his father had read together. A sultan's tent, maybe. Or in the Days of Yore, with knights and giants and people eating whole turkey legs for breakfast. He hoped they would not still be in Downriver, where turkey was just for Thanksgiving and the only knights were plastic ones you got with purchase at Guinevere's Pizza and Subs.

If he were a real knight, Milo thought, then his dad would probably be a knight too. The two of them would be heroes, riding black steeds through dark forests together, fighting ogres, and swearing oaths. His dad would not have to worry about Mr. Tuckerman's assistant, or go on business trips like he had this week, and Grandmother—who wasn't even his real grandmother, but a live-in babysitting lady Tuckerman

Fencing provided and paid for—could go back to wherever it was she came from and Milo would never again have to tell a spot from a dot.

This is what he was thinking when he reached into the laundry basket and pulled out a sock that was neither spotted nor dotted. Nor was it navy blue. It was, in fact, yellow and as large as the Christmas stockings that Milo had seen decorating the Uptown Shopping Center. It was much larger than his father's foot. Larger, even, than Grandmother's.

But it must be Grandmother's, Milo thought, *and there must be a second one.* He flipped the contents of the basket onto the carpet and sifted through the dots and spots. There was no other yellow sock.

Maybe it's still in the dryer, he thought, and down he went into the damp of the basement, where the washer and dryer sat on a tall wooden platform he and his father had built to keep the appliances from shorting out when the basement flooded, which it did most every time it rained.

Milo opened the dryer door and reached into the dark of the machine. He felt nothing, not even the back of the dryer. He was too short.

He was always too short and, in the words of Grandmother, scrawny.

To her this was a blessing, for although Milo was far too old for the styles offered in the Barely Boys section at the department store, he was still small enough to fit the largest sizes offered there. Few boys beyond kindergarten age would be caught dead in puppy dog pants or yellow duckling sweatshirts, of course, and the largest of the Barely Boys clothes tended to linger on the racks and then go on sale at a significant discount. That is when Grandmother—who loved a bargain—bought them and brought them home to Milo. He saved the most humiliating outfits for weekends and snow days and other times when none of his classmates would see him. Since it was the first day of Thanksgiving break, Milo was wearing one such item now, the aforementioned yellow duckling sweatshirt. The ducky sat smack in the middle of his chest. It had googly eyes and said *quank* if you pressed it.

Not even quack, thought Milo. *Quank.*

He stood on his toes and reached farther into the dryer, but again felt nothing.

An inch of platform stuck out from under the machine. Milo got a toehold there, gripped the dryer opening, and pulled himself up. Again he reached in and again he felt nothing. He tucked his head inside, leaning his chest against the opening to gain a few inches.

Quank, complained the ducky.

Milo thought he heard a faint ripping sound and checked the seat of his corduroys. If he had split them, Grandmother would be livid. He found no tear, but his relief was fleeting, for he knew she'd be just as angry if he didn't locate the missing yellow sock. He waved his hand around inside the dryer. Nothing. No, wait—something. Something woolly and damp. The missing sock, of course. What else could it be? Milo tugged at the sock.

And the sock tugged back.

"Ack!" yelled Milo. He let go of the sock and tried to heave himself out of the dryer, but the sock, or whatever it was, was too quick. It clamped on to his hand and pulled him all the way in.

The dryer door slammed shut behind him.

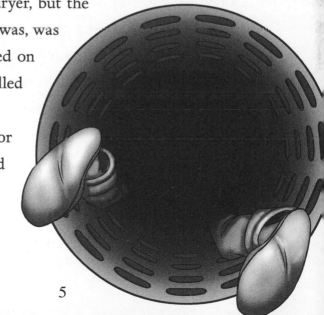

2

There's Your Problem

For a very long while, Milo felt as if he were being dragged downward, and then for a long time after, he had the sensation of being pulled up and then, finally, out.

"There's your problem, ma'am. Ya got a boy wedged in here."

"A boy? Heavens! How did that get in there?"

"Can't say, ma'am. Used to be, dryers just got jammed with all them tiny socks coming from who-knows-where, but with these SuperDry 200s? When they ain't exploding, we're finding boys in 'em. Don't worry, this one's out now."

The boy in question was, of course, Milo, who was at that moment dangling by his wrist, which was pinched between the thumb and forefinger of a very large, very hairy, very sour-smelling sort of someone. What was going on? Had he shrunk in the dryer? Grandmother had told him such things happened to sweaters and fine linens, but he had not considered the possibility that people might shrink as well.

"You didn't happen to find a baby bootie in there too, did you? A yellow one?"

"Just this boy," said the sour fellow, shaking Milo as if he were a tiny bell. Milo did not ring, but he did consider throwing up. "You want I should dispose of him?"

Dispose of him?

"Drop him in there, won't you? I'm sure my husband will want him for tea."

A sweaty hand closed around Milo, blocking his view and making it even more difficult to manage the short panicky breaths he now realized he had been taking.

"He ain't that big what'll satisfy."

"I'll take him just the same."

The hand opened, and Milo glimpsed an enor mous kitchen counter, orderly and clean, with a row of large porcelain jars set upon it, each labeled in

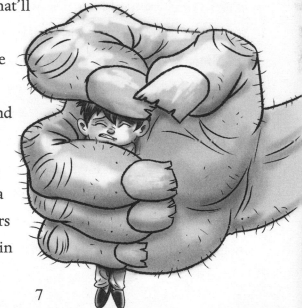

cheery cursive letters: SUGAR and FLOUR and ROADKILL and
BOYS. He guessed his fate and was right. The lid was lifted off
the BOYS jar and he was dropped inside. Before he could get
to his feet, the lid was replaced and Milo was left in the dark.

The dark, as it turns out, was not such a horrible place
to be. Or maybe it was horrible, but it had its usefulness, for
there in the dark Milo had nothing to look at and was thus
able to replay what had just happened and try to sort out the
details of it all. It was quite unbelievable. Moments ago, he
had been sock sorting, and now here he was on the kitchen
counter of a . . . well . . . of a someone. A large someone.

Milo had gotten a glimpse of her. She was enormous —
so tall, he figured, that she'd need to crouch to fit into the
gym at his school. Her arms and legs were thick as telephone
poles, and a dense tangle of ginger hair sprouted along them.
A similar shade covered her head, which was round and so
disproportionally large that its weight would likely have

snapped her neck in two, should she have had much of a neck at all. She wore a housecoat, much like Grandmother's, and glasses — the old-fashioned sort that made a person want to call them spectacles.

She had been holding something that Milo had initially registered as a woolly ham, but seeing as that made no sense at all, he revised his recollection to think of it as a baby. Yes, it must have been a baby, for the hairy woman had held it to her shoulder and patted it once or twice, which is hardly the sort of treatment one would expect a ham to receive.

As if in reply to his conclusion, Milo now heard a muffled cry that could only belong to an infant or a goat. *I'm nearly positive I did not see a goat,* Milo thought, although a goat might explain the peculiar smell of the place.

It struck him then that whether or not he had seen a goat was rather beside the point. He was in a canister on a counter in who-knows-where. What had happened? Where was he? Milo felt his head for lumps. Did he have a concussion? Was he dreaming?

The crying reached a higher pitch and was soon joined by the dull sound of humming. It was that "Hush, Little Baby" tune that Milo's mother used to sing. Mom had changed the words, telling the baby in the song not to snore, an alteration that allowed her to rhyme her name, Eleanor, and remind Milo that she would love him "forever more." How long had it been since he had heard her sing? Certainly not since she left last year, but before that, how long? Two years? Three?

The song outside the canister continued, now with lyrics that varied greatly from both the standard and his mother's version.

"Hush, little headache, don't make a peep;
Mama won't be happy till you're fast asleep.
And if you cannot sleep, dear soul,
Mama's going to feed you to a mountain troll."

Milo found the song unsettling, but the baby was soothed by it. A grating whine replaced the infant's full-on wail.

"What is it, Woodchuck?" Milo heard the woman say. "What do you want? You want a biscuit? A biscuit? Is that what you want?"

Woodchuck increased the volume of his cries. He did not want a biscuit.

"A rock? A rubber band? Chopsticks? Savings bonds?" Woodchuck did not want any of these things either.

"Oh! I know what you want. You want this." An

earthquake struck, or that's how it felt to Milo, but it was simply his canister of temporary residence sliding across the gleaming countertop and into the meaty arms of the woman. A moment later, the lid lifted and Milo squinted in the light.

"Daddy would not like hearing that I let you play with his food, but I won't tell if you won't," the woman boomed.

Woodchuck must have agreed, for once again, Milo felt himself pinched and lifted. The shaggy woman held him at nose level. He was no bigger than the glasses on her face. She sniffed and shuddered. "Disgusting," she said. "But if this will keep your daddy from noticing that you have misplaced yet another bootie, then I suppose it's worth it."

Milo was deposited onto a long table in front of the drooling baby, who made a grab for him. "No, Woodchuck," said the woman. "Dirty. Dirty little boy. Don't touch."

At first Milo was resentful. He had bathed just yesterday and, since his father had left the bottle on the counter, had put on a splash of aftershave as well. He was not dirty, and he did not smell disgusting. Still, if such an opinion would keep him out of the drooly hands of young Woodchuck, he knew he ought to be pleased by the description.

"Do something, boy," said the woman. She repeated it

slowly and loudly—"Do. Something."—as if Milo were daft or hard of hearing.

"What should I do?" he asked.

"You talk? Don't talk. Oh, don't talk." The woman shuddered again. "Gives me the willies." She wrung her hands. "Dance or something. Juggle. My great-aunt told me she had a boy one time who could juggle. She did say he ended up being salty and tough, though, didn't she? Don't juggle after all. Dance. Can you dance?"

Milo had been to a wedding once and had avoided dancing as much as was possible. The flower girl had noticed him, however, and had dragged him under the disco ball to engage in something she called "the chicken dance," which involved flapping one's arms like wings and making beaks of one's hands. Milo danced the chicken dance now as baby Woodchuck giggled and blew a bubble out his nose.

"That's better," said the woman. "You just keep dancing. I'm going to search for that bootie upstairs."

The woman turned and left, each step shaking the room and causing Milo to stumble this way and that, mid-chicken. The shaking diminished once she was finally up the stairs, and Milo recognized the moment as his chance for escape. He glanced about the room.

There was a door to the outside, but it was closed and most certainly would be too heavy for him to budge. The window above the sink was closed too, and besides, it was much too far away. In the center of the table stood a salt-shaker and a pepper mill, each approximately half Milo's height and far too narrow to hide inside. At the distant end of the table, farthest away from Woodchuck, sat a newspaper, the *Ogregonian*. "All the News We Feel like Printing" it said at the top.

What they felt like printing, Milo discovered as he danced down the length of the table and over to the paper, was a picture of someone nearly as hairy as Woodchuck's mother, wearing a turtleneck and a terrifying smirk. The headline read:

**HOME OFFICE TO UNVEIL NEW DRYER TOMORROW!
CEO DASHMAN SAYS:
"THANKS TO RECLUSIVE GENIUS DR. EL,
THIS ONE DON'T EXPLODE!"**

"Gicksle!" snorted Woodchuck. "Snnyiiiiiiiiiiiiiiiiiiiiiiiiiiii."

"Keep dancing!" hollered the woman from upstairs. Milo flapped his arms and wiggled his hips. Maybe, he thought, he could tear a page from the newspaper. He could fold it like a paper airplane and sit in it and fly down to the floor.

It was not a brilliant idea, admittedly, but Milo was in a bit of a panic and found it difficult to hatch a plan and chicken-wiggle simultaneously.

He returned his attention to the newspaper, careful to keep dancing as he plotted out the best way to tear the page. And that is when he noticed another, much smaller photograph at the bottom corner of the paper. Above it was a headline:

OGREGON'S MOST WANTED CRIMINAL CAPTURED!

Ogregon? *So this hairy woman and her baby are ogres,* Milo thought. *Wait—there are ogres?* How could that be? There were ogres in the books he had read, sure, but not in real life. And this was real life, wasn't it? He was a real kid. And this was a real room. And a real newspaper.

Citizens of Ogregon is gonna rest easier tonight knowing the legendary outlaw Tuckerman that has been terrorizing everybody has been caught by officials and is being held at the Home Office home office in an upside-down bucket with some holes punched in it.

"He can't get out," said Chief of Security Growl Magnesson. "We put a rock on there."

Tuckerman? Like Dad's boss, Mr. Tuckerman? Of Tuckerman Fencing? Of course, that couldn't be. *But how weird,* thought Milo.

Woodchuck snorted.

"Dancing, boy!" came a holler from above.

Milo flapped and continued reading.

Officials are still hunting for Tuckerman's right-hand man, known only as Tuckerman's Right-Hand Man.

"An inside source says he's gonna show up and try to rescue Tuckerman before the Squashing," said Magnesson. "But we'll be ready for him. He won't escape this time."

Citizens are told to keep an eye open for Tuckerman's Right-Hand Man, though nobody knows what he looks like.

The only photo that exists of this dangerous criminal is below. The *Ogregonian* is sorry for the lousy quality. The photographer dropped his camera. He has been sacked.

The photograph was, indeed, lousy. The shot was most likely taken just as the camera hit the floor, for it was angled in such a way that Tuckerman's Right-Hand Man's shoe—brown, plain, and indistinct—took up most of the frame.

But Milo was not looking at the shoe. Milo was looking just above the shoe and just below the pant cuff, between which flashed an inch or so of sock. A dark sock. With light spots. Or dots. Milo was not sure which. But he was sure of one thing.

The sock belonged to his father.

3

Toboggan-esque

What is my father—a door-to-door fence salesman—doing on the front page of the Ogregonian? thought Milo. What he should have been thinking, of course, was what was *he* doing on the front page of the *Ogregonian,* for indeed, Milo was standing there on the newspaper, not dancing, not planning his escape, but standing there, stunned by the sight of his father's sock.

If he had read the article correctly, Mr. Tuckerman was about to be "Squashed" (which did not sound good) and a security ogre was making plans to capture Dad (which also sounded pretty bad).

I've got to warn him, Milo thought. It was a very brave thought, considering that at that exact moment Woodchuck had begun howling again and the ogre woman was thundering down the stairs hollering for Milo to continue his chicken routine.

It was also at that exact moment that a loud banging could be heard at the door.

"Shut up, Woodchuck!" shouted the woman. She thudded past the table, shaking it so violently that both Milo and the pepper mill toppled. Woodchuck giggled and sneezed a sneeze so wet and drooly that even though Milo stood on the far end of the table, he instinctively curled into the crouch-and-cover position he had learned for tornado drills at school.

"You again," said the woman as she opened the door.

"I called the Home Office." Milo recognized the voice as belonging to the sour-smelling ogre who had first pulled him from the SuperDry 200. "They say that in order for you to get your refund, I godda bring in the offending article, what is that boy."

"You've got to be kidding," said the woman. Woodchuck howled louder.

"Them is my orders, ma'am." The sour man pushed his

18

way into the kitchen. Focused as he was on the last place he had seen the boy, he failed to notice Milo huddled on the *Ogregonian*.

The repairman wore a red jumpsuit with the words HOME OFFICE REPAIR: IF WE CAN'T FIX IT, YOU SHOULD PROBABLY BUY A NEW ONE FROM US printed on the back. Around his waist was a tool belt from which dangled a predictable clatter of wrenches, screwdrivers, and hammers, as well as a magnifying glass, a large drawstring nail pouch, and what appeared to be an enormous banana.

"First I godda disable your dryer, what I already did, so no worries about it exploding you. Yours is one of the last SuperDry 200s in all of Ogregon. Me and Floyd got the assignment this morning. There was five dryers left, and between us, we got 'em all destroyed up. Floyd found a boy too. His bites. Anyway, our orders is we godda bring 'em in." The repairman lifted the lid of the BOYS jar and peered inside. "Hey. He ain't in here."

"He ain't?" The ogre woman thudded over and pretended to look inside the canister. "My, my. He ain't. Well, then. Where could he be?" She turned her back to the table, where Milo now sat. "Maybe you put him in the wrong jar. Look in the others."

The repairman reached for the jar marked SUGAR and looked inside. Or at least, that was what Milo assumed had happened. He could not actually see this occurrence, for just at that moment a large dinner napkin dropped from the sky, knocking him flat onto the *Ogregonian* and covering him completely.

"Where could he have gotten to?" said the woman. "Where oh where oh where?"

Milo heard cabinet doors opening and drawers slamming. He lifted the edge of the napkin and peeked out. A hairy finger smooshed against his face, pushing him back under the cloth. "No, no, no," said the woman.

"No, what?" asked the repairman.

"I'm talking to the baby. No, no, no, Precious. No . . . no doing what you're doing . . . over there." Woodchuck sneezed

again. Milo was reminded of the time he and his father had gone tent camping in the rain and was grateful for the cover offered by the dinner napkin.

"He ain't nowhere, lady." The repairman sounded as if he might cry. Woodchuck did cry.

"Shut up, Woodchuck!" said the woman. Woodchuck cried louder. "I guess the Home Office will just have to trust that you found a boy in the dryer."

"The Home Office ain't the kind what trusts." The repairman sat heavily on the far corner of the table nearest the wailing baby. The table tilted perilously under his weight. "I am gonna be sacked."

Milo lifted the napkin again. The fallen pepper mill had begun rolling down the table's now-slanted surface, spinning faster and faster until it flew off the edge, smacked hard against the cupboards, and crashed to the floor. Peppercorns could be heard rolling to all corners of the kitchen.

"I am the world's stinkingest repairman!" sobbed the repairman. Woodchuck harmonized. The ogre woman yelled for the both of them to shut up and thundered off to the closet for a broom.

It was quite a din, and under normal circumstances, Milo might have been found with his fingers in his ears, but these were not normal circumstances. First, Milo did not want to be found at all. And second, his fingers were already occupied, clutching desperately to the *Ogregonian,* upon which he was now slowly slipping, toboggan-esque, down the slope of the kitchen table.

Toboggan-esque?

Yes. Toboggan-esque.

Milo felt almost exactly as he had the afternoon last winter when his father had taken him sledding. A surprise snowfall had canceled school and made the roads impassable for even the most dedicated of door-to-door fence salesmen. Grandmother had called them lunatics, but Milo ignored her, following his father outside into the snapping cold. They had dragged a toboggan through the freezing drifts to the small shopping-center home of Guinevere's Pizza and Subs, behind which stood the steep, snow-covered hill that separated Downriver from the much more well-to-do city of Uptown.

The hill was very steep, and Milo had doubted his ability to climb it. But Dad had been so sad and distracted since Mom had left that Milo could not bear to disappoint him now, when he looked joyful and carefree. Instead, Milo stepped carefully into the tracks his father made, using his mittened hands to climb when necessary. Finally, panting and sweaty, they reached the pinnacle. It was a long way down.

His father had held the toboggan steady. "Everything you need is right here," he said, patting Milo on the sternum. "Lean left to go right. Lean right to go left. Drag your boots to slow down."

Milo felt the toboggan shift underneath him. "Aren't you coming with me?" he asked.

"I'm always with you," said Milo's father. And then he let go of the sled.

Lean left to go right, thought Milo, flipping himself into a sitting position. The dinner napkin still covered his face, but he knew that straight ahead and to his left was the edge of the table and then the abyss. To the right, however, sat a formidable repairman backside. If Milo could steer to the right, he would crash into that backside, and though he might have a different sort of trouble ahead, at least he would not suffer the smashing fate that the pepper mill had. Thus, Milo leaned left.

The *Ogregonian* shifted course and picked up speed. *Drag your boots to slow down,* Milo thought. He pushed his feet hard against the tabletop, but it did no good. Grandmother did not allow shoes to be worn in the house, and as a result, Milo was not wearing boots; nor was he wearing sneakers or even fancy dress shoes. Milo was wearing slippers, which were now living up to their name.

"Figures," said Milo.

"Whee!" yelled Woodchuck.

Crack! The *Ogregonian* smacked into the saltshaker, spinning a half turn. Milo was now sledding backwards.

The saltshaker barreled past. Milo heard it rumble off the edge of the table and shatter on the floor. An image of himself meeting the same end flashed through Milo's mind, his broken body splattered on the *Ogregonian,* right beside the photo of his father's sock.

His father! If Milo died here, Dad would never know what had happened. It was bad enough that Mom had taken off for California or Paris or wherever she was. Milo couldn't just disappear, leaving his father to wonder if he had done something to chase his son away.

Lean right to go—no, wait. Milo was going backwards now. *Lean left to go right.* He leaned hard to the left. *Bam!* His head cracked against the repairman's hammer.

Figures, thought Milo dizzily. *Why couldn't I have smacked into the banana?*

"Snsooxkkk!" Woodchuck waved his arms so wildly that his highchair threatened to topple.

The repairman reached to steady the chair. "Lady, you'd better—"

"I think it is *you* who had better," said the woman, setting down her broom. She clapped a hand over her infant's wet mouth. "You've done nothing but make a mess and inflame my child. OUCH! Woodchuck! No biting!"

"Snkkkseesn!" insisted the baby.

"I ain't got the boy." The repairman sniffed and wiped his nose on the sleeve of his jumpsuit. "I can't leave without him. My wife will kill me if I lose another job."

"Tell her to send me an invitation to the funeral," said the woman. And with that, she pulled the repairman to his feet, escorted him to the door, and shut it firmly behind him. "Let's see to tea," she said.

Thus, the ogre woman turned to see to tea, but instead saw the napkin-covered *Ogregonian* tilting, tipping, and then tumbling off the edge of the kitchen table and down, down, down to the cold hard floor below.

4

The Plan

"Drat," said the woman. The boy was probably broken now, and her husband would not have the pleasure of smashing him for tea. "Are you broken, boy? No, don't answer. Don't talk." She lifted the dinner napkin and peeked underneath.

Milo was not there.

She shook the napkin.

Milo did not fall from it.

She looked under the *Ogregonian* and in the BOYS jar and behind the busted pepper mill.

Milo was not in any of those places.

Milo had escaped.

"Sneeeeeeepthhhhh," said Woodchuck. He had seen it happen. While his mother swept peppercorns from the kitchen corners, the tiny boy had slipped out from under the napkin and folded himself into the fat leather pouch that hung from the repairman's hip, pulling the drawstring closed behind him. Woodchuck had tried to inform his mother of the boy's hiding place, but she had only smashed her hand over his mouth and hollered. And when she slammed the door—hard—the boyless newspaper had toppled.

"Snee," said Woodchuck, shaking his head sadly.

"Shut up," said his mother.

Milo heard none of this, for he was on the Ogregon Turnpike, inside a Home Office repair truck, inside the repairman's nail pouch, huddled upon what he assumed was an industrial-sized sponge.

He had anticipated finding nails and other pointy things inside the pouch and had lowered himself slowly, certain he was about to be impaled on a wood screw. Instead, his feet found something soft and springy. To make himself less visible, Milo had curled into a ball upon the sponge and pulled the pouch's drawstring tight. It was not until then that he noticed the smell: a powerful, eye-stinging smell, a cross between Grandmother's depilatory cream and a hamster cage.

Milo's eyes adjusted to the dark of the pouch. He saw sesame seeds.

He was not resting upon a sponge at all.

He was curled atop a half-eaten turkey sandwich, which had, by the moldy looks of it, been deposited there more than six days ago and sat waiting, land-mine-esque, for someone to discover it.

That someone was Milo.

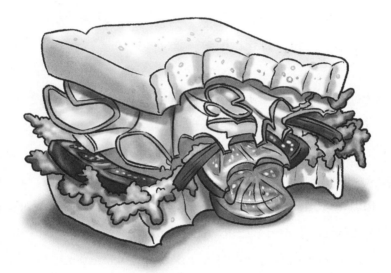

"Figures," he said, holding his nose. His eyes watered.

It was the smell, he told himself. He was not crying, even though he had every right in the world to cry. He had nearly fallen to his death and had narrowly escaped being served for tea. He had felt so clever, escaping from the ogre kitchen as he had, but now he was no better off than before. Maybe worse. When he had first seen his father's sock in the *Ogregonian,* he had been flooded with heroic thoughts—he'd warn his father of a dangerous plot and the two of them would escape together. But now Milo realized how foolish those thoughts had been.

He didn't know where his father was.

He didn't even know where *he* was.

It came to Milo that his best chance of returning home would probably have been to climb back into that ogre lady's dryer. Instead, here he was cowering on a rancid sandwich, trapped in a sack, being transported who-knew-where by a subpar repairman. All he could hope was that the repairman would stop to fix something else. Then, maybe, he could crawl away and look for an escape route. But what about Dad? Dad would still be here, in Ogregon, heading straight into danger . . .

Milo wiped his eyes. As if in response, music filled the Home Office truck. It was the twingy-twangy sort that Grandmother listened to while she made her supper. He could almost hear her now, warbling out the call letters of her favorite radio station, WSAD, over the hum of the microwave.

"Holy crap, I need a nap, 'cuz I'm so tired of you," she'd sing.

Milo knew not to interrupt while Grandmother was singing. Not for sock-sorting advice or homework help or even to tell her she had set the microwave for twenty minutes again, instead of two like the macaroni box instructed. It was better to wait, even if it did mean he'd have to clean up the exploded macaroni later. His scrawny fingers were so much smaller than hers, Grandmother would say. It was easier for him to reach into all the grooves and corners.

Once, Milo had protested. "It's not my mess," he'd said.

"Life is full of messes that aren't yours. That doesn't mean you don't have to clean them up," said Grandmother, and then she had gone back to singing.

"Boy, your neediness is tedious.
I need a nap, 'cuz I'm so tired of you."

Twingy-twang. The song on the repairman's radio was just as sad-sounding as Grandmother's.

"I'm sick of eating turkey, I'm sick of fricassee.
Boiled or baked or corny-flaked, don't feed more bird to me.
I've had my fill of turkey hash, à la king, and cordon bleu.
There's only one thing I want to eat. Listen up and I'll tell you:
a boy, a boy, a human boy with ketchup on the side.
Such tender meat, such spicy feet, such crunchy bones inside."

Milo shuddered.

He did not want to think about his bones being crunchy.

He did not want to think about his feet being spicy. His eyes teared up again. Darn moldy mayonnaise.

He needed fresh air, was all. Slowly, Milo released the drawstring and poked his head out of the pouch as the song continued:

"If you love me, darlin', like you ought to,
put your hairy hand in mine,
and vow you'll cook me up a boy
with crunchy bones inside!"

A deep voice sounded from the truck radio. "I couldn't agree more. It's half off the hour, Ogregonians, one thirty, and I got your traffic and weather reports. Traffic stinks. Weather: Put your head out the window and check, if you're so dang curious. And now for a classic from way back in '08, 'Gravy Boat Blues.'" A guitar moaned, and a gruff voice sang out.

"I dreamed the most delicious dream
of boys to chop and chew . . ."

Milo did not want to think about being chopped and chewed any more than he wanted to think about being crunchy and spicy. He looked around for something to distract himself. The truck in which he now sat was a boxy one, much like that of the ice cream vendor that sometimes raced through Downriver on its way to Uptown. From his tool-belt perch, Milo could see to the vehicle's spacious back compartment, which was filled with boxes and tools and replacement parts. It was separated from the cab of the truck by a shiny metal wall on which were taped various Home Office announcements.

ALWAYS PRETEND THE CUSTOMER IS RIGHT, read a bright yellow flyer.

The wall was also home to a diagram of the SuperDry 200, the very dryer from which Milo had been recently extracted.

". . . an elbow would be swell, though.
All I got is the gravy boat blues . . ."

Milo concentrated on the diagram. Back home, Grandmother was always knocking over toasters or applying excessive force to the television remote, and Milo had developed a knack for fixing things. Once, after a basement flood, Dad had even taken the back off their clothes dryer and showed Milo how to replace a few of its shorted-out wires.

Although the SuperDry 200 was at least six times the size

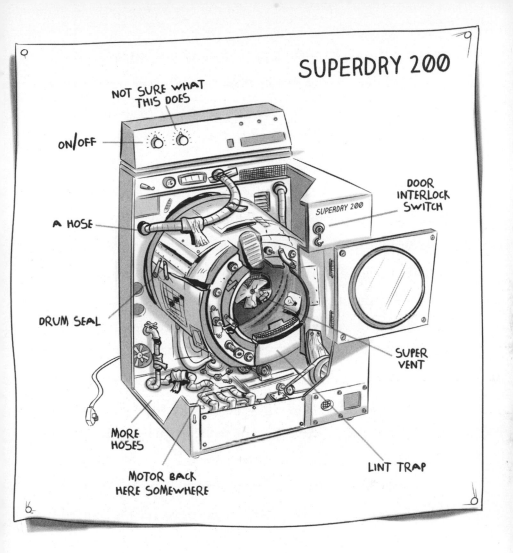

of the dryer in Milo's basement, the basic construction was similar: a tumbler mechanism turned the barrel; hoses and vents controlled the flow of air. Unlike the dryer at home, however, this one seemed to be built of spare parts, and there were a great many gaps and holes where neither gaps nor holes should be. Between the dryer door and the lint trap, for example, was a space so wide and deep that Milo figured he could fit inside it. *No wonder SuperDry 200s are always exploding,* he thought. A gap like that would make the lint trap useless. It didn't take a mechanical genius to see how dust, threads, and paper bits would slip right under the trap and clog the air vent behind it. When the dryer got hot enough, all that trapped lint would catch fire and then, well, *boom!*

"I interrupt this Roy Ogreson classic with important news," said the radio announcer. "Just a second. Let me get my glasses."

A clattering sound rattled through the speakers, followed by a terrific thud. "I'm all right. I'm aaaaall right . . . Just hold on, I'll find 'em . . . You'll want to hear this. It's about the Tuckerman Squashing this afternoon . . ."

This afternoon? Milo's heart pounded. The newspaper he had seen on the ogre woman's table must have been from yesterday. Which meant that his father was in danger of being caught *today.*

"Here they are. Bling-blanged bifocals. Okay, then. Shut up out there and listen." The radio announcer cleared his throat and read, " 'Citizens of Ogregon: Get out of the road. You guys are clogging up Main Street and making it so nobody important can get anywhere. The Officials of Ogregon is working with the Home Office so that the ones of you with a television that works can see the Squashing on it at . . .' Just a second . . . Myra? Is that a five or a six? You sure? You got the worst handwriting, I swear . . . Okay, 'five o'clock—' "

Five o'clock? But hadn't that announcer just said it was one thirty now? How was Milo supposed to find Dad in just three and a half hours?

"So, watch your TV and don't come downtown or nothing. Also, the mayor has dibs on Tuckerman for supper, so don't think you can hang around and get some carry-out. Now go home."

I wish I could, thought Milo. *I wish I could.*

5

The Home Office
Home Office

The Home Office truck shuddered to a stop. Milo ducked back into the pouch as the repairman began the slow, sad walk to his fate.

Slow and sad as it might have been, it was also extraordinarily bumpy. With every step, Milo was jostled and bounced like a ship on rough seas, and his stomach threatened mutiny. Bits of moldy sandwich crumbled beneath him. Spoiled mayonnaise soaked his corduroys, and flecks of sour turkey clung to his ducky shirt. The scent was overpowering. Desperate for fresh air, Milo poked his head out of the pouch once more. Immediately, he dove back inside.

There were ogres everywhere.

Ogres in dresses, ogres in suits, and, here and there, ogres in red Home Office jumpsuits like the one his repairman sported. Milo could hear them now too. Bites of conversation filled his ears as ogres jostled past.

". . . so I says to him, if you don't like it, don't eat it, and he says . . ."

". . . not at the court house, at the Home Office, so they can show them Big Wigs that new dryer doodad . . ."

". . . did you ever have boy? My uncle had a kneecap once. Just a kneecap. Says it was the most delicious . . ."

Milo would have plugged his ears if doing so would not have required him to let go of his nose.

Finally, the repairman made a sharp right turn, and in a matter of steps, the chatter ceased. Milo peeked out again. The repairman had left the crowded sidewalk and was approaching the side entrance of a shiny marble building. Before the doorway stood a crooked sign, the words on which started out large and impressive but grew smaller and more cramped as the sign maker appeared to have run out of space: THE HOME OFFICE HOME OFFICE. MAKER OF EVERY-THING IMPORTANT, EXCEPT CARS AND THOSE THINGS YOU USE TO KEEP YOUR BASEMENT FROM GETTING DAMP. DELIVERIES: USE BACK ENTRANCE. CUSTOMER COMPLAINTS: GO HOME AND CALL US ON THE TELEPHONE. BUSTED TELEPHONE: BUY A NEW ONE.

The repairman pulled open the door and stepped inside.

. . .

And so it was that Milo entered the Home Office home office —the very place the radio announcer had said Mr. Tuckerman's Squashing would occur. The very place, Milo knew, he was most likely to find his father.

But how? Before them lay a long, dimly lit hallway with what seemed like hundreds of doors, each with a frosted-glass window. As the repair ogre shuffled along, Milo regarded each door hopefully. OFFICE OF SHAVING TECHNOLOGY, said a sign on one window. OFFICE OF TELEPHONES, read another. He wished they would come across one that read, OFFICE WHERE MILO'S FATHER IS HIDING.

A few of the doors stood open, and Milo peeked cautiously inside as the repair ogre passed. Tall tables and walls of equipment filled the rooms. Milo was reminded of the lab he had visited on "Celebrate Science Day" at Uptown High School, except that instead of pimply-faced teenagers in safety glasses, these rooms housed lab-coated ogres tangled in wires or hurling toasters.

The repairman continued down the corridor. The floors, Milo noticed, were sparkling clean, but nearly anything that could be busted, bent, or broken, was. Wall clocks and exit signs dangled hangman-esque from frazzled wires. In the ceiling fixtures, burnt-out bulbs outnumbered their operational neighbors by a factor of three. A battered drinking fountain hung spoutless on the wall, a damp and misspelled OUT OF ODOR sign taped upon it. A matching sign was affixed to a nearby elevator, the doors of which seemed to have resigned from their duties before closing completely.

Where would his father be? Was he in one of these offices? Was he already rescuing Mr. Tuckerman? And what was Mr. Tuckerman doing in Ogregon anyway? It was difficult to imagine even the tallest Tuckerman fence being useful to an ogre.

The repairman turned a corner, passing two more empty offices before reaching a third, which was anything but. To the contrary, the bustle inside the Office of Bragging About Stuff was so extraordinary that the repairman was compelled to stop and stare. Milo did the same.

The room was filled with ogres — some in lab coats, others in sparkly costumes or business clothes. There were ogres positioning lights on tripods and others fiddling with television cameras. Still others hovered around a bank of front-loading washing machines that lined the far wall, slamming doors that stubbornly popped back open at the slightest provocation. At the front of the room was a tall wooden lectern and a silvery screen like the ones at the Uptown Cinema, although the image upon it bore no resemblance to the *Test Your Movie IQ* slides that so annoyed Milo at the theater back home. Across this screen was projected an illustration: a fat pilgrim-worthy turkey and a similarly plump human boy.

"Dr. El wants him Squashed *after* the announcement, right?" hollered a camera ogre. "I don't wanna go in for no close-up and get guts on my equipment."

This was it! This was where Mr. Tuckerman's Squashing was going to happen!

Milo searched the room frantically for any sign of his father, but saw nothing. That made sense, of course. His father would be hiding, waiting to make his move. Milo fought the urge to call out. What he really needed to do was get out of this pouch—but how? He'd break his neck if he jumped, and surely he'd be noticed if he tried shimmying down the repairman's pant leg.

There was nothing he could do.

Figures, thought Milo.

It was never like this for heroes in books.

Milo had read lots of books with his father before Mom had gone away. Back then, it was Mom who traveled for her job—often for months at a time. Milo had missed her, of course, but had gotten used to it, and Dad had made everything okay. Every day, Dad had picked him up from school and made him supper and helped him with his homework. And every night, without fail, his father had read him stories of adventure and magic and derring-do. Dad would pull a chair up beside Milo's bed and open their book across his lap. His voice would grow warm and soft, and the whole house would seem to quiet with him, the creaky floorboards and rattling furnace and humming appliances hushing themselves and leaning in to listen.

All that changed last year, when Mom left and didn't come back. First, Dad started working late into the night and on weekends. Then Grandmother moved in to be with Milo when Dad was away, which happened more and more often. Ever since, Milo had taken the bus to school and cooked his own macaroni and cheese for supper and muddled through his homework alone. He never complained. Dad seemed sad and tired enough, and besides, there was nothing to do about it. He knew Dad couldn't afford to hire a sitter on his own, and Grandmother was what Tuckerman Fencing had provided. So, Milo did his best to clean up after himself and do his chores, but all it took was a pair of boots left where they shouldn't be for Grandmother to mutter how it was no wonder his mother had needed to get away from it all.

Milo tried not to think about whether Grandmother was right about his mom. He tried not to miss his dad. It was hard, especially at bedtime. And so every night as the light slipped away from the day, Milo slipped under his covers and opened one of the books he and Dad had shared, imagining his father's best storytelling voice as he read each line.

If only he could hear his father's voice now, narrating his current situation. What would Dad say? *The small boy looked out of the soggy, smelly pouch . . . and did nothing.*

"Hey, you! Where do ya think you're going?"

Milo dropped back into the pouch, pulling the drawstrings as tightly as he could. Despite his efforts, a gap remained through which he could see a significant patch of Home Office home office ceiling.

"I'm going to get sacked," sniffed the repairman.

"Not in the Bragging Office, you ain't." A shadow slid across the pouch opening, and a hulking figure passed slowly overhead: first an arm, then the words HOME OFFICE SECURITY stitched across a shaggy brown sweater (at least, Milo hoped it was a sweater), then ceiling again. "This area's reserved for Big Wigs, which don't include you."

The sweater came back into view. *He's circling,* thought Milo, though just as he thought it, the sweater stopped moving. The security ogre leaned forward. Milo saw a bulbous nose, upon which sat mirrored glasses like the ones favored by the police officers on Grandmother's favorite TV show. He watched as the reflection in the lenses moved from the red of the repairman's jumpsuit to the glinty silver of his hammer to a small patch of eye-popping, attention-grabbing yellow.

Duckling-sweatshirt yellow.

"What we got here?" A hairy palm hovered over the pouch. Milo closed his eyes and felt a yank on the tool belt. This was it. He was lunch.

"Hey!" protested the repairman.

Milo opened his eyes. He was still in the pouch. Above him, a shaggy paw clutched a banana.

"Snacking on the job is against regulations," said the security ogre, pointing the fruit like a pistol.

"I'm going to get sacked," sobbed the repairman. "How much worse can a banana make things?"

"I am confiscating this." The security ogre grinned. "I'll just put it in here for safekeeping." Milo watched as the grin split, revealing a horrifying row of jagged gray teeth. In three sharp bites, the banana was eaten—peel and all. "Now," said the security ogre. "Go get sacked."

The repairman did as he was told, shuffling and sobbing down the long Home Office hallway. Milo, having no choice in the matter, was carried along with him, and though he did not cry, he could not help but feel like doing so, as each ogre step took him that much farther from the place he felt certain his father was most likely to be.

6

For Crying Out Loud

The repairman had sobbed through the entire thing. From the moment he entered the Office of Ogre Resources, through the time he was relieved of his tool belt and jump-suit, to when he was escorted out of the office, he had sniffed and moaned and lamented. He could still be heard wailing long after the door had closed behind him.

Milo might have been sympathetic were he not feeling equally distraught. He was still in the foul-smelling pouch, which had been dropped along with the repairman's tool belt onto the desk of a secretarial ogre Milo had heard referred to as Grace. The repairman's jumpsuit had been tossed atop the tool belt and as a result, Milo once again found himself in the dark, straining his ears for the footfalls of additional ogres or the licking of chops.

He heard nothing. The Office of Ogre Resources was empty.

Now's my chance, he thought for the second time that day, and once again he wondered just what sort of chance he thought he had. He was a small boy in a big world, and every time he got some tiny sense of where he was in it, everything changed.

He was in the building where the Squashing was going to happen, he knew that much, and he was pretty sure he knew the room where it would take place too—that Office of Bragging About Stuff. If his father was really going to rescue Mr. Tuckerman from being Squashed, it would probably be in that room. His best chance at finding his father, Milo figured, was to get back there—and soon. But how? A slab of moldy turkey gave way under his knee.

Step one, he thought, *get away from the sandwich.*

Milo wriggled from his nail pouch hideout and peeked out from under the jumpsuit. The Office of Ogre Resources looked a lot like the main office of Downriver Elementary, except that where his school secretary had hung inspirational posters coaching students to GET READING and KEEP CALM AND CARRY ON, someone had taped up less encouraging thoughts. GET LOST, advised one. KEEP CALM AND CARRION, said another.

Step one accomplished. But what's step two?

A kid in a story would know exactly what to do. He'd race to the edge of the desk, scurry to the exit, and wait for some preoccupied ogre to come by and open the door. Then he'd dash out into the hallway and down to that Bragging Office and probably save a whole bunch of other people and defeat all the bad guys and then his beaming-proud father would show up and they'd all go home.

I bet if that story kid had seen a security ogre bite through a banana peel, he'd be a little less quick with his super-fancy plans, Milo thought. But he couldn't just stay hidden under the jumpsuit, either. Eventually he'd be discovered, and then what?

With a deep breath, Milo prepared to escape. "One . . ."
he whispered to himself. "Two . . . Thr—"

"Oh, for crying out loud!" A voice like a rusty hinge
pierced the air. "What time is it? Two o'clock? I swear, you
can't leave for five minutes without somebody dropping
junk on your desk." Milo froze as the claws of the ogre he
assumed to be Grace snatched the note that had been left for
her.

"Escorted off the premises? Ha! Went to McGobbler's is
more likely." A terrible crackle filled Milo's ears, and he imagined the irritated ogre pulverizing the note in her fist. He
tried very hard not to imagine what his bones would sound
like in similar circumstances, an effort made infinitely more
difficult as he, the tool belt, and the Home Office jumpsuit
were swept off the desk and into the ogre's arms.

"Ooof! Don't they ever wash these things? For crying out
loud!" Grace sniffed. "This one smells like . . . like . . ."

Like boy, thought Milo. *I'm doomed.*

". . . like week-old turkey!"

Milo mouthed a silent thank-you to the sandwich as the
revolted ogre clomped out of the Office of Ogre Resources
and into the hallway beyond. If Grace took a right, she would

retrace the steps the repairman had taken, bringing Milo closer to the Office of Bragging About Stuff and, he hoped, his father.

Please take a right. Please take a right.

Grace took a left.

Figures, thought Milo, twisting a wayward jumpsuit thread around his fingers.

The secretarial ogre trudged down this hallway and that, each step taking Milo farther from the place he longed to be. He calculated the minutes it took—five, maybe? How long would it take him to make the return trip on his own? How many Milo strides would equal a single ogre step? How was he ever going to get to the Bragging Office in time to find Dad and go home?

Keys jingled and a lock clicked. Milo felt Grace shove open a door. She took two more steps, and the door slammed shut behind her.

"For crying out loud, where'd that light switch go?" The secretarial ogre stumbled and the tool belt shifted in her arms. Suddenly, as though perched upon a newly sprung trapdoor, Milo fell from Grace.

This is it, he thought as he plummeted. *The end.*

He winced in anticipation of the splat he knew was to

come until, with a jolt, his floorward progress was abruptly halted. The jumpsuit thread with which he had been fiddling was tangled around his fingers, and Milo now dangled, marionette-esque, in the dark.

The repairman's hammer, which had also slipped from Grace's grip, had no such tether and cracked loudly on the floor below.

"For crying out loud." The irritated ogre stooped to search for the hammer, and as she did, Milo's slippers touched the ground. He shook his hand to free it, but the thread, having worked itself into a complicated series of knots, stayed in place. Milo pulled. The knots tightened.

Milo ducked as Grace's enormous hand swept past to pat the ground beside him. Any second now he would be discovered and no doubt eaten faster than a repairman's banana. How many bites would it take? he wondered. Three bites? Two . . . *bites!*

Quickly, Milo bit into the thread, but his

teeth—being of a less razorlike quality than a security ogre's —had barely found purchase when Grace located the hammer. She stood, and again Milo was airborne, suspended now by his teeth. *Banana,* Milo reminded himself. He ground his molars.

Ba . . .

na . . .

na . . .

Snap! Milo fell through the darkness, landing on his belly with a *quank.*

"For crying out—?" The secretarial ogre slapped the wall several times and then—*click!* A light buzzed on overhead. Milo found himself flanked by a pair of sensible ogre shoes, hidden from Grace by her own considerable girth.

They were in an enormous supply closet. Generations of office supplies, busted electronics, and cleaning gear were stuffed onto metal shelves that skyscrapered along the walls. Milo scanned for hiding places among the dinged-up buckets and broken typewriters. He found plenty, but getting to them would require dashing across the closet floor and into the secretarial ogre's view.

Behind him, however, pushed not-quite-flush to the wall, sat a stout wicker clothes hamper that looked to Milo to be the size of a small moving van. Scrambling to his feet, Milo darted for it, wedging himself into the crevice between wicker and wall. The weave of the basket was loose, and if he angled his head just right, he was able to see through its many small gaps.

Grace hurled the tool belt onto one of the closet's higher shelves. Milo held his breath as she turned to lift the hamper lid and drop the sacked repairman's jumpsuit inside.

"There," she said, letting the lid slam closed. "How difficult was that?"

It was the sort of question Grandmother often asked when it came to putting away bath towels and army men, so even if it had not been asked by a petulant ogre, Milo would have known it was a question best left unanswered. Had he attempted a reply, he would not have been heard anyway. A thunderous voice was booming from outside the closet door.

"Put him down and come out with your hands up!"

Put him down? Milo's heart, which seemed to have been beating double-time since he had been pulled from the SuperDry 200, now quadrupled its pace.

"What *him?*" screeched Grace.

Me him, thought Milo.

The ogre on the other side of the door waited for

neither screech nor thought. With a deafening *crack!* the door exploded off its hinges. Sticky notes, staplers, pushpins, and packing tape rained from the shelves and clouds of dust mushroomed as the door thwacked to the floor, a hulking security ogre splayed across it.

"Oh, hello, Gracie," he said, when the last box of paper clips had clattered to the floor. "Don't you look nice today?"

The ogre secretary coughed and patted her hairdo. "Roger, you big luggy-lug. The door wasn't even locked."

"It wasn't? Dang." Roger got to his feet. "Bet you wasn't gonna steal Tuckerman, neither."

"Tuckerman!?" gasped Grace, her hairy hand fluttering to her heart.

Tuckerman? thought Milo. *He thinks I'm Mr. Tuckerman?*

"You're still in here, ain't ya, Tuckerman? Ohh, Tuuuuuuuckerman!" Roger laughed and stomped his foot, rattling the supply shelves and raising a fresh tornado of dust.

Milo felt a tickle in his nose. He couldn't sneeze now. Not now.

Do not sneeze, he told himself. *Do not sn—aaaaaaa AAAAAAHHHHHHHH-CHOO!*

Grace screamed. "What was that?"

Milo steeled himself to hear the security ogre explain

about the boy she had inadvertently carried with her into the supply closet. What he heard instead was a sharp, disdainful voice that sounded very much as if it were coming from the inside of a cave.

"It was a sneeze, you dope."

7

Tuckerman

"Manners, Tuckerman," snarled the security ogre, squeezing past Grace to squat beside a trio of mops in the far corner of the room.

"Tuckerman is here?" cried the secretarial ogre. "In my supply closet?

"It's okay, Gracie. Look, I got a rock on there."

It was then that Milo noticed it. Next to the mops sat an overturned cleaning bucket with a rock atop it. There were three small holes punched in the bucket.

Mr. Tuckerman. The real Mr. Tuckerman, his father's boss, was being held prisoner right here in this very supply closet! Milo looked around. What if Dad was here too? What if Dad was here and hiding, waiting to come to Mr. Tuckerman's rescue?

"I told you to call me Tuck," echoed the voice in the bucket.

"I could have been . . . anything could have . . ." Grace sputtered. "How come you weren't on guard?"

From his spot behind the hamper, Milo could not be sure, but he thought he saw Roger blush.

"Might I could be on TV later. You know, at the Squashing and the demo? I wanted to call my mom and tell her, so's she could watch, but I couldn't find a phone that works."

"I got a telephone in my office, you luggy-lug." Grace held out her hand. "How about you come use that?"

Milo was certain Roger was blushing now.

"But what about Tuckerman?"

"Tuck," corrected the bucket voice.

"There ain't practically nobody left in the building except them show-offs in the Bragging Office," cooed Grace. "Who'd notice you snuck out for a itsy-tiny phone call?"

Roger took the secretarial ogre's hand. Together they lifted the splintered door, balanced it against its

frame, and, giggling, headed away down the long Home Office corridor.

Milo stepped out from behind the hamper. "Dad?" he whispered. "Dad, are you in here?"

There was no answer.

Dad was probably still on his way. Maybe he was creeping down an air duct or along some secret passage right this second. Maybe he would come racing in and rescue Mr. Tuckerman just in the nick of time. If that were true, Milo thought, then perhaps it would be a good idea to get a little closer to where Mr. Tuckerman was, so that his father wouldn't have to race around to rescue Milo, too. Maybe they could even rescue Mr. Tuckerman together.

Before she left, Grace had slapped off the light, but because the door no longer fit tightly in its frame, there was enough illumination spilling in from the hallway that Milo could still see the silhouette of the upside-down bucket. He picked his way toward it, careful to avoid the thumbtacks and paper clips that littered the floor. He did not want Mr.

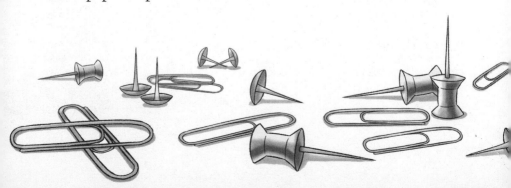

Tuckerman to think that his Right-Hand Man had a clumsy doofus for a son.

"Mr. Tuckerman?" Milo whispered. He knocked politely on the bucket. "Mr. Tuckerman?"

"Tuck," said the voice. "Surely you got the memo?"

"Memo?"

"Never mind. Go ahead."

"Go ahead?"

"Are you repeating everything I say, or is there some bucket acoustical issue going on?"

"Bucket acou— No, not . . ." Okay, maybe Mr. Tuckerman *would* think his Right-Hand Man had a doofus for a son. "Sorry," said Milo. "I'm not sure what you mean."

"By acoustical?"

"By go ahead."

"With the rescue."

"The rescue—"

"There it goes again!"

Doofus, Milo thought. *Super doofus.*

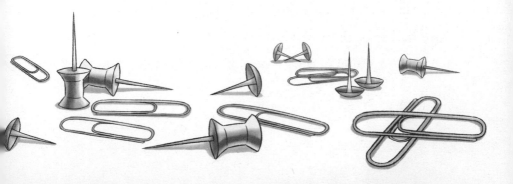

"I hadn't noticed any echo when that security idiot was chatting me up," continued the voice. "Anyway, I thought Lyndon would come for me himself, instead of sending . . . Well, you must be pretty good. You did find me, right?"

"Right," said Milo. Except, of course, that it was not right at all. He hadn't really *found* anyone. He had been carried around first by one ogre and then another, arriving in this supply closet completely by chance. Still, Mr. Tuckerman didn't have to know that.

"So, go ahead."

Fine. He would go ahead. Maybe he could get Mr. Tuckerman out from under the bucket before Dad showed up. There'd be no way Mr. Tuckerman could think he was a doofus then. Maybe he'd even clap him on the back and tell Dad what a clever young man he had for a son. Maybe he'd give Dad a raise. Maybe Dad wouldn't have to work so many hours and could be home more, like before.

Maybe they could even get rid of Grandmother.

Milo studied the bucket as best he could in the dim closet light. It was at least twice his height, and, as the security ogre had said, there was a rock on there. Nonetheless, Milo worked his fingers under a dent in the bucket lip and tried to lift it.

"If it was that easy, I'd have done it myself," said the voice. "Are you really one of our best? I guess Lyndon was right about the need to weed."

Milo considered the challenge once again and was reminded of last year's history unit on the great pyramids. Egyptian conscripts had used a system of pulleys and levers to lift and move two-and-a-half ton blocks of stone. Unfortunately, Milo had discovered, there were rarely any conscripts or pulleys around when you needed them. He did not have a lever, either, but perhaps, he thought as he scanned the closet floor, he could build one.

"I've got an idea," he said.

"Nifty," said the voice. "I'll be sure to put that in your evaluation."

Milo thought he detected sarcasm, but chalked it up to bucket acoustical issues and went on with his plan. Among the rolls of masking tape and bottles of window cleaner that had fallen from the shelves were two dozen pink erasers. Milo stacked them, pyramid-esque, near the base of the bucket. That would serve as the fulcrum. Now all he needed was a lever. A nearby yardstick proved heavier than he imagined, but with a great deal of grunting and sweating, he dragged it into place, wedging one end under the dent in

the bucket lip and balancing the remainder upon the eraser pyramid. All he had to do now was add weight to the far end of the yardstick and, like a schoolyard seesaw, the short end would rise, the bucket lip would lift, and Mr. Tuckerman would be free.

Milo stepped up onto the yardstick and, step after careful step, made his way up its steeply angled slope. Finally, as he neared the very last ogre inches, the lever dipped. He looked over his shoulder and was rewarded by the sight. The bucket lip had lifted just high enough to reveal Mr. Tuckerman's knees.

"Mr. . . . um, Tuck? Can you crawl out?" Milo called.

"*Crawl* out? That's the plan?" The voice, still echoing in its bucket prison, sounded annoyed.

It wasn't a particularly elegant rescue, it was true. There

were no galloping horses or flashing swords or cheering crowds of adoring villagers, but still, Milo had thought his father's boss might be a little happier about it.

"Fine," said the voice. "Just a second."

Milo had never met Mr. Tuckerman, but he had always imagined him to look something like the principal at Downriver Elementary—tall and broad chested, with gray hair cut army short and a ruddy face that always looked slightly sunburned. Perhaps it was the angle from which Milo was looking or the limited light, but the Mr. Tuckerman that Milo saw crawling out from under the bucket appeared much smaller than Principal Plutschuck. He had more hair, too, and wore it long enough that as he crawled to freedom, it covered his face completely.

"You're not here." The voice behind the hair sounded less deep than it had inside the bucket, but at this moment Milo cared little for pitch and much more for content. Was it possible that it had been so dark under the bucket that Mr. Tuckerman's eyes were still adjusting to the dim supply-closet light?

Milo made his way down the yardstick. "Yes, I am," he said.

Mr. Tuckerman remained on his knees, head down,

attention focused not on Milo, but on a glowing rectangular device he held in his hand. "You are not." He patted his jacket pockets, found what appeared to be an identical device, and consulted it as well. "You're not here, either."

As much as Milo wished Mr. Tuckerman's statement were true, and that he were anywhere but here, here was where he was, and Milo was beginning to resent that Mr. Tuckerman would say otherwise. After all, if he wasn't here, Mr. Tuckerman would still be trapped in a bucket. Milo opened his mouth to say so when the tiny man leaped to his feet and strode away, waving the shiny devices in the air.

"There's no signal from Headquarters, but the Tracker should be working. As long as an agent is carrying his or her ZoomBaby, it will show up on the Tracker. Like Lyndon says, a good agent *always* carries his or her ZoomBaby. Thus, you are either not a good agent or . . ." Still holding the devices overhead, Mr. Tuckerman turned in Milo's direction.

Which is when, for the first time in that darkened room, each noticed something startling about the other. They voiced their observations simultaneously:

"You're just a kid."

8

Just a Kid

Just a kid?

Yes, just a kid.

Equally shocking to Milo, the person he had formerly thought of as Mr. Tuckerman appeared to be a girl. A dark-haired, freckle-faced, not-very-happy-to-have-been-called-a-kid girl.

"You're not Mr. Tuckerman," said Milo.

"And you're not one of our brightest, are you?" The girl hooked her hair behind her ear and gave Milo a down-the-nose look that seemed to suggest superiority—though it was possible that she had simply caught a whiff of his mayonnaise-soaked footwear. "I can't believe Lyndon would allow some shrimpy trainee kid to go out on a mission involving the Head of the Tuckerman Agency. Are you undercover?

Is that why you're out of uniform? What division are you from?"

What was this girl talking about? "I—I'm not from any division," stammered Milo. "I'm from Downriver."

"No, you're not. Unless you mean the Fencing Office? And if so"—ZoomBaby still in hand, she thrust an index finger an inch from his nose—"how did you get here?"

How could Milo explain? He wasn't exactly sure how he had gotten there himself.

It turned out not to matter, however, as the girl did not pause for an answer. "I suppose it's okay just this once. Go ahead, finish up." She brushed a fleck of dust from an impressive-looking medal on her jacket. "But don't think this will get you your job back. All of you in the Fencing Office have been let go. Permanently. Had to do it—"

Let go? "My dad works for Tuckerman Fencing," said Milo. "Samson Speck?"

"Speck. Yes. Well." The girl returned her attention to the ZoomBaby screen.

"Yes, well, what?" asked Milo.

"It's classified. All personnel matters are classified. But, since you're his son . . . I'll just say that Samson Speck was particularly difficult. He came rushing to Headquarters,

66

demanding to talk about why I had fired him and what my *father* would have wanted, and . . ." She peeked at Milo warily. "Well, there was a bit of a scuffle. A mix-up. This one was his." She waggled one of the ZoomBabys. "It doesn't have a signal either. The records are okay and the games work. The recorder is fine."

The girl tapped the screen. "Hello?" she said into the air.

"The recorder is fine," the machine repeated.

"See? Voice-activated replay works too. It's just the signal. I can't connect with the network. If I could, then Lyndon would know where to find—" The girl stopped abruptly. She looked at Milo as if seeing him for the first time. "Wait. Hold up. You're saying Lyndon didn't send you to rescue me?"

"Who's Lyndon?" asked Milo.

The girl squinted accusingly. "If Lyndon didn't send you, why are you here?"

I wish I knew, thought Milo.

A door closed somewhere far down

the hallway, and Milo was reminded that any second now the security ogre would complete his call to his mother and return to the supply closet.

"We've got to hide," Milo said.

"Oh, do we?" asked the girl. "Tell me, do you know how to get me back to Headquarters?"

Milo shook his head. "I don't even know what Headquarters is," he admitted.

"Then *you* hide, and I'll wait here for someone who does know. I am the Head of the Tuckerman Agency, after all. *Someone* will come for me. It says so in the manual. It was nice meeting you, Junior Speck. Now, on your way."

Milo knew nothing about any manual, but he knew he needed to hide. He also knew that as much as he might want to, he couldn't leave this Tuck girl loitering outside her bucket. As soon as the security ogre saw her, it would be obvious that she'd had help escaping. How long until that ogre started searching the place for an accomplice?

"Okay," said Milo. "You're right. Someone's coming to rescue you. But you don't need to hang out here next to the bucket for that, do you?"

The girl considered this. "I guess not. And Lyndon *would*

be impressed to hear I'd evaded my captors. Do you think the reinstatement board would too? I mean, it's not like I did something horrible in the first place. Just a little mermaid research for a Halloween costume. How was I to know those snotty fish kids wouldn't cooperate?"

"I don't know," said Milo, because he didn't. He didn't understand anything the girl was saying.

"And it could be good publicity," she continued. "How about this: 'New Tuckerman Leader Escapes from Ogre Prison Single-Handedly'?"

Milo considered pointing out that there were at least two other hands involved in the operation, but decided against it.

"Okay, I'll hide. But"—she waved her ZoomBaby at the makeshift lever—"don't you think this thing is sort of a giveaway that something's up?"

Milo rushed to dismantle the fulcrum, hurling the erasers as far from the bucket as he could. Tuck kicked at the yardstick, but otherwise

continued pacing about the closet, arms raised in search of a ZoomBaby signal.

"You know, that security ogre will figure out I'm missing as soon as he starts talking," she said. "He just loves to chat. 'None of the girls ever notice me. This is my chance at a promotion. I wonder how you'd taste with honey mustard sauce.' Blah blah blah. When I don't answer, he'll know I'm gone." Tuck tapped another button on the screen.

"Blah blah blah," repeated the ZoomBaby.

An idea struck. "Your little computer thing—" said Milo.

"ZoomBaby," corrected Tuck.

"Your ZoomBaby. You said it has voice-activated replay?"

"It's a very useful function for large presentations. You can program it to say 'Hear! Hear!' when you finish a sentence, or respond when it senses a question, so if you don't feel like listening to someone, you can—"

"That!" said Milo. "That's what we need! Could you say a bunch of stuff into it now? We can set it to play when it hears a question. We'll slide the ZoomBaby under the dent in the bucket, and then, when the ogre starts talking—"

"I get it, Junior Speck, I get it. It's not some elaborate twelve-point plan to reinhabit the Northmost Orcan Province, is it?"

Milo had to agree that it was not.

"All right, then." Tuck turned her back and spoke into the ZoomBaby while Milo rushed to drag the yardstick back to the spot where he had found it.

"Ready?" he asked Tuck when he returned.

Tuck put a finger to her lips. "It's all set," she whispered. "Programmed. Activated. Under the bucket."

Just at that moment, footsteps sounded outside the door.

"Does this plan of yours include running?" asked the girl.

It did.

9

Nobody

Milo and Tuck had just slipped behind the hamper when the supply-closet door was lifted from its frame and Roger the security ogre stomped back inside.

"You still here, Tuckerman?" he called.

"This is ridiculous," replied the ZoomBaby.

"I guess it is sort of ridiculous." Roger sat cross-legged beside the bucket and propped his chin thoughtfully upon his shaggy fist. "All the Big Wigs, the fancy show."

It worked! His plan had worked! Milo wanted to cheer but, in the interest of remaining silent and undiscovered, turned to give Tuck a thumbs-up instead. Tuck, however, did not return the gesture, as her thumbs were already occupied in the decidedly thumb-dependent task of scaling the side of the Home Office hamper.

"What are you doing?" Milo hissed.

"Altitude, Junior Speck." Tuck waved her remaining ZoomBaby. "May be able to catch a signal higher up."

On the other side of the hamper, the burly ogre sighed thoughtfully. "I'd just make a sandwich of you myself if it wouldn't get me fired, you know?"

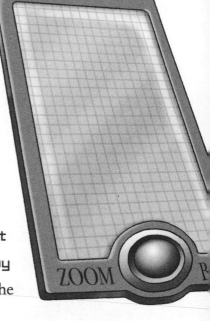

"Twelve hours under a bucket and who shows up? A shrimpy kid with no training at all," said the ZoomBaby.

"Hey, I've had training," said Roger. "I just need to apply myself—that's what my mom says. Between you and me, though, Tuckerman, I don't think I'm cut out for security. My real dream is to be a singer-songwriter."

"And what's his big plan? Record yourself."

"Recording?" Roger chuckled. "Now, that's flattering. I mean, you haven't even heard one of my numbers. But, you know . . . if you wanted . . ." He tapped a bluesy rhythm on the overturned bucket, cleared his throat, and began to sing:

"My toaster has exploded,
my dryer's on the fritz.
I wanted to call you and tell you, my darling,
but my telephone called it quits . . ."

While the security ogre sang, Tuck climbed higher. Milo watched as she paused every few steps to wave her ZoomBaby in the air. As annoying as she might be, he had to admire how focused she was on her goal.

Milo, on the other hand, felt so unfocused he was practically dizzy. Nothing made sense. After reading the *Ogregonian,* he had expected to find his father's boss, Mr. Tuckerman, inside the bucket, not some girl. But the girl had said *she* was the Head of the Tuckerman Agency, and even though Milo had never heard Dad refer to Tuckerman Fencing as an agency, it was pretty clear that Tuck was his father's boss. After all, she had fired him.

Wait.

She had *fired* his father.

"My appliance reliance has kept me sad and blue.
I'm worn and I'm broke and I'm busted
and my television set is too."

Roger howled and the supply shelves rattled. The hamper

shuddered too. Milo looked up just in time to see Tuck's foot slip, her leg plunging thigh-deep through the wicker wall.

Serves her right, thought Milo.

"My electric razor's done shocked me like a Taser.
I'm woozy and I'm just coming to.
I'm stunned and I'm scratchy,
and my beard is kinda patchy.
Tell me, darlin', do you taste metal too?"

"What in the deep-fried drumstick is going on in here?"

Milo ducked farther behind the hamper. A second ogre had appeared in the supply-closet doorway. He was skinny and bent and wore a blue Home Office jumpsuit, much like the one the repairman had sported. The badge on his chest was larger than the repairman's had been, and two attempts at spelling the word MAINTENANCE had been stitched and crossed out before the badge maker had settled on writing JANITOR instead.

Roger leaped to his feet. "I'm guarding Tuckerman."

"Don't think you're supposed to torture him like that."

"I was singing. Tuckerman likes it, don't you, Tuckerman?"

"Wasting my time with a nobody," said the ZoomBaby.

The janitor cackled. "Called you Nobody, Tuckerman did."

"Get out," growled the security ogre.

"Bragging Office needs laundry, Nobody."

"Get it and get out of here. And can you make it snappy?"

The janitor, still chuckling, reached for the hamper. Milo froze. What if the janitor opened the hamper and saw a tiny leg poking through its wicker wall? He and Tuck would be caught for sure.

"Only reason I'm even doing this is because I feel sorry for him," said the ZoomBaby.

"Ha-hahaha!" howled the janitor. "You tell him, Tuckerman! Tell that Nobody what's what!"

Roger's face purpled. "Get out!" he roared. "Take the basket and get out!"

Milo grabbed hold of the wicker just in time. With a grunt, the janitor lifted the hamper and, by extension, the two children clinging to it. He carried it into the corridor and dropped it onto a rickety trolley full of cleaning supplies and trash bags. "Godda get going, Nobody!" called the janitor. "Will you miss me, Nobody?"

Roger howled again, but somehow Milo was still able to hear the ZoomBaby's response:

"I wish Lyndon were here instead of this stupid kid."

Milo still had no idea who Lyndon was, but at that moment, he wished it too.

10

Any More Questions?

Once, Milo had visited a joke shop and had gotten stuck in what the shopkeeper called Chinese handcuffs, though the man admitted that there was nothing Chinese about them and that, in fact, they were manufactured in Vietnam. The "handcuffs" didn't even cuff one's hands but instead formed a woven tube, into which Milo was told to insert his index fingers. "Now try pulling your way out of 'em," said the joke-shop man.

Milo followed instructions, pulling with all of his might, but his efforts only tightened the trap. It was not until he pushed his fingers together that the weave loosened and he was freed.

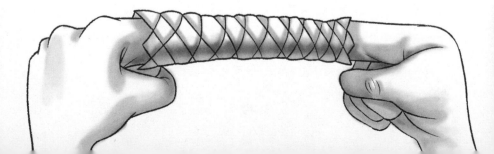

"Try pushing your leg in deeper," said Milo when he had climbed the hamper wall high enough to reach the wicker-wedged Tuck.

"Ha, ha," said Tuck. "Try pushing your head up your—"

"I'm not kidding. Try it."

Tuck tried, and the hamper loosened its grip, creating just enough space for Milo to slide his fingers into the gap and hold the opening wide. Rather than being pleased, however, Tuck removed her leg from its woven prison with visible resentment. She was equally resentful when Milo suggested they find a hiding spot among the trolley's array of cleaning supplies and trash bags.

"What's the matter?" Milo whispered. Although the clank and rattle of the trolley was enough to cover even the loudest conversation, he was taking no chances of being overheard.

Tuck, however, spoke in the same Head-of-the-Tuckerman-Agency voice she had employed since exiting her bucket prison. " 'What's the matter?' A wicker deathtrap nearly cuts off my leg. I'm no longer anywhere near the spot where Lyndon would look to rescue me. I'm the Head of the Tuckerman Agency, but some kid who knows how to make seesaws thinks he can boss me around. I'm tired. I'm hungry.

I want to go home and"—she felt the back of her suit pants —"I think I sat in vanilla pudding. Any more questions?"

Milo had hundreds of questions. What was this Tuckerman Agency, and how had his dad—a door-to-door fence salesman—been a part of it? And what was with the ogres? He had always believed that ogres were creatures of books and legends, but here he was in a land stuffed full of them. Were they real? How had he gotten here? Where exactly was "here"? But as the girl beside him wiped the pudding from her suit pants, he could tell it was an unlikely time to receive a helpful answer.

The janitorial trolley rattled down yet another hallway. Like the one Milo had seen upon entering the Home Office home office, it was lined with countless doors leading to countless offices. He read the door signs as they passed: OFFICE OF IRONS (CLOTHES, CURLING); OFFICE OF REFRIGERATORS; OFFICE OF LAMPS (DESK, FLOOR, HEAD, BUT NOT MAGIC, BECAUSE THERE AIN'T NO SUCH THING, SO STOP ASKING).

"Is too," said Tuck, who had looked up from her ZoomBaby. "Lyndon says that a lot of the Aways don't believe in magic. All they see is their regular life and they don't understand there's magic in it. They just call it normal."

"What's an 'Away'?" asked Milo. Perhaps he would receive a civil answer to a topic Tuck had brought up herself.

"This is an Away. Ogregon. All the troll villages and sirens' coves and banshee communes, those are Aways too. All the places that aren't Home," said Tuck. "Of course, for an ogre, this is Home and the place where we live is an Away, but you get the idea."

Milo did. Sort of. "So, how come we're here?"

"I don't know how come *we're* here, Junior Speck. I know how come *I'm* here. I'm here to get my privileges back. "

"Your privileges?"

"You've got a real problem with that echo thing. You ought to see a specialist. My privileges. My . . . certain things I can't do at the moment." Tuck waved the ZoomBaby as if shooing a fly.

"Why not?"

"It's classified," said Tuck. The whiff-of-sour-slippers look had returned to her face. "No big deal. Lyndon said they'd be easy to get back. All I had to do was prove to the reinstatement board that I could handle a mission. And so we came here. A quick turnaround, it was supposed to be. Testing a network issue. But then something happened and we got separated and one of those ogre idiots found me and picked me up and I said to put me down, that I was Head of the Tuckerman Agency, and he started hopping around singing about how he had caught Tuckerman. I told him I wasn't Tuckerman, that I was Tuck. That Tuckerman was my father. That he had, um, died, and I was . . ." She turned her attention back to the ZoomBaby.

"I'm sorry to hear about your dad," said Milo. "I didn't know."

"We kept the news strictly inside the Agency. It would make the transition easier, Lyndon said. Anyway, it was a year and a half ago. I got used to not having a mother after she died, and it's not like my father was around that much . . . I'm fine. Fine. Excellent, really." Tuck polished the medal on her jacket. "So, what I was saying? Oh, yeah —ogres don't see well, as you may have noticed, and they're dopes. They don't notice if we are boys or girls or even how old we are. As far as they were concerned, they had caught Tuckerman. Thus: Bucket. Plans for Squashing. Then you, dragging me away from the spot where Lyndon was sure to find me."

Tuck inspected her medal again. It was thick and shiny and glinted in the hallway's dim light. "Nice, huh?" She angled it toward Milo so he could see the writing engraved upon it: EXCELLENCE.

"What'd you get it for?" asked Milo.

"Excellence, obviously." Tuck shook her head as if he was no smarter than an ogre. "You know, just, excellence. Lyndon gave it to me."

"So Lyndon is your boss."

"*I* am the boss. Lyndon is . . . he used to be my father's assistant. Second in command, Lyndon called it. He took care of everything at Headquarters, all the administrative work, the planning, the marketing, and, when I wasn't away at boarding school or summer camp, me. When my father died, I was next in line to take over, and I kept Lyndon in the position. I am the Head of the Agency, but Lyndon is like—"

Milo had a sudden sick feeling in his stomach. "—like your Right-Hand Man."

"I'm left-handed," said Tuck.

"No, I mean . . ." Milo remembered the photo he had seen in the *Ogregonian*. "This might sound weird—but, does Lyndon wear socks with spots on them?"

83

"Dots," corrected Tuck. She lifted a pant leg to reveal a dark sock with small, pale dots. "Everyone in the Agency wears them."

And just like that, Milo knew. The picture in the *Ogregonian* had been Lyndon, or someone else who worked at the Tuckerman Agency.

Hearing that his father had been fired probably should have convinced him, but it hadn't. Seeing Tuck's sock had.

Dad was not in Ogregon.

11

Bragging About Stuff

The trolley swerved around a sharp corner and into a corridor that Milo could not fail to recognize. There were the two dark offices he had seen earlier, and there was the Office of Bragging About Stuff, the very busy ogre-filled room where Milo knew the Squashing was scheduled to take place.

Earlier, when he had believed his father was somewhere in that room waiting to rescue Mr. Tuckerman, it was the only place in all of Ogregon that Milo had wanted to be, but now that he knew differently, he wanted nothing more than to pass by undetected. He pulled a bit of trash bag farther over his head and crouched low.

Keep going straight, he willed the janitor. *Keep going straight*.

The trolley turned and pushed through the Bragging Office doorway.

Figures, thought Milo.

The room was filled with lights and cables and folding chairs and two dozen squabbling ogres. A squat ogre woman in red-framed glasses and a black beret stood behind the lectern at the front of the room, shouting and waving as if signaling a passing ship. "Where's the script?" she hollered, tearing the beret from her head and hurling it to the ground. "Where are the dancing girls? Who's in charge here?"

A mousy-looking assistant retrieved the hat, then whispered into the angry ogre's ear.

"Oh, right," she said, slapping the beret back into place. "*I'm* the director. *I'm* in charge here!"

The janitor's trolley came to a stop in front of the bank of washing machines Milo had spotted earlier. He could hear the hamper lid being lifted and dirty clothes being gathered. "Goodbye, Nobody, I says to him," muttered the janitor. "Ha!"

Milo peeked out from under the trash bag. A scrum of ogres had collected near the lectern, elbowing and shoving as the director shouted instructions. At the back of the room, where the janitor's trolley sat, it was quieter. Equipment cases and coils of television cables were strewn about, but there was not a single ogre anywhere near, aside from the janitor, who was busy shoving the hamper's contents into one of the washers. All they had to do, Milo thought, was keep quiet and hidden, and pretty soon the janitor would wheel them away from the Office of Bragging About Stuff and off to, well, who knew? Wherever it was, it had to be better than this room full of ogres.

Milo's thoughts were interrupted by a sharp poke to his rib cage.

"Look," said Tuck. She held up her ZoomBaby. A silver grid spanned the screen, in the middle of which was a fat red dot. Two tiny dots hovered at the far edges of the grid.

"Is that a game?" Milo asked in a whisper.

"It's the Tracker," said Tuck. "It shows any other ZoomBabys in the area. That red dot in the middle is ours, and the small one that isn't moving is the one under the bucket."

"My dad's," said Milo.

"I've been able to see those since I got here. But this one is new." She tapped the second small dot, which Milo could now see was moving slowly closer to the fat red one. "I *told* you someone would come. If I could connect to the main network, the ID function would work and I'd know if it was

Lyndon, but that's another ZoomBaby, for sure. There's an agent coming for me."

Emphasis, Milo could not help but notice, had been placed on the word *me*. "Of course," Tuck continued, "I'll order him to rescue you, too. Wouldn't look as good to the reinstatement board if the Head of the Tuckerman Agency left behind a helpless victim."

"Helpless?" Milo couldn't believe this girl. He had to remind himself to whisper. "Who got you out from under a bucket? Who pulled your leg out of the hamper?"

"Actually," continued Tuck as if he had not spoken at all, "Lyndon probably brought an entire rescue team." She stood up and looked around.

"What are you doing? Someone's going to see you!"

"It will be easier for the team to find me if I'm not rolling all over Ogregon with sacks of garbage, won't it?" she said, making her way to the edge of the trolley and lowering herself over its side. "Coming?"

What choice did he have? Milo crawled to the side of the

trolley just in time to see Tuck scale a coil of television cables and drop down inside it.

"Now what?" he asked once he had joined her.

"Quiet!" yelled the director. "QUI-ET!"

The room fell silent. The only sounds were the buzz of the spotlights and the sullen *chugga-chug* of the newly started washing machine

"WHO TURNED THAT ON!?" The director shouted so loudly that every ogre in the room jumped. *Sproing!* The washer door flew open and a waterfall of hot, bubbling suds spilled onto the Office of Bragging About Stuff floor.

The black beret sailed across the room. "Washers don't run till the demo! Somebody turn that off! Somebody get a mop! Somebody call maintenance!"

"I'm right here!" hollered the janitor. He was unable to mop up the mess, however, for the steamy water had fogged his glasses so completely that he could not see a thing. Like-wise, the soapsuds made walking a slippery affair. A single

step, and the janitorial ogre was sliding across the room and into a row of folding chairs.

The director waited for her beret to be returned to her and threw it again. "This is a disaster!" she cried. "Somebody call security and stop them from bringing Dr. El down here and seeing this mess!"

Ogres scrambled into action, sliding on soapsuds and crashing into one another as they competed to find a working telephone. Finally, a phone was acquired and the message was relayed.

"All right!" hollered the director. "Run-through! All non-essentials, out!" For a moment no one moved, each ogre believing him- or herself to be as essential as the next, but eventually the room was emptied of all but those operating cameras, aiming spotlights, or wearing shiny costumes. The last to leave was the janitor, who, after waiting several minutes for his glasses to defog, had finally succeeded in drying the floor.

"Hit the lights on your way out," commanded the director.

The room went dark, aside from the light that shone from the hallway through the half-open door.

"SPOTS!" With a *pop!*, two bluish lights cut through the dark to illuminate the lectern, where the director stood blinking. "Right. So, here's how it will go. CEO Dashman comes out, applause. He introduces Dr. El, applause."

"You mean we're finally gonna get to see Dr. El?" said an essential ogre.

"Of course you're gonna get to see Dr. El, you idiot. All of Ogregon is gonna get to see Dr. El. That's why we got cameras. Everything you see here"—the director slapped the large silver screen—"is what's gonna be on TV. Including the mysterious Dr. El."

A growl of conversation rumbled through the darkened room.

"You seen Dr. El yet?"

"Nope."

"Not me."

"Nobody has, except Dashman and a couple of security guys."

"I heard the security guys ain't even allowed to look."

"SHUT UP!" The director's assistant was already in

motion when the beret whizzed through the spotlit air. He caught it midflight and returned it to his boss's head before she had even finished yelling. "Right. So. The big-shot scientist blah blah blahs, only one who knows how this whazzit thingy works, yadda yadda yadda. We bring out the whazzit. Make a big deal about it being the only one in existence, so complicated that only genius Dr. El can make it, yadda yadda. Applause. Then the slide show."

The words *Out with the NOISE, in with the BOYS!* appeared on the screen behind the director, along with a crooked photo of the clothes dryer from which Milo had been pulled earlier that day. Where a logo had once proclaimed SUPERDRY 200, someone had used a marker to add another zero.

"The SuperDry 2000! Applause." The director waved her hands as if quieting a cheering crowd. "No more fiery explosions, thanks to . . . next slide . . . the whazzit!" A new image filled the screen. The whazzit was silver and shiny and shaped like an enormous wedge of cheese. At its narrowest point, Milo could see a hinge.

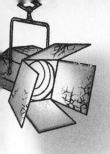
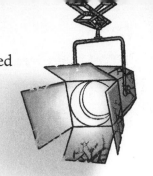

"Next and next!" hollered the director. A third slide showed how the hinge opened, drawbridge-esque.

A row of hooks sprang out, like claws on a cat's paw.

"Dr. El talks some more. Nobody understands a word," continued the director. "Yadda yadda, applause. Cue the music."

A fanfare echoed in the room.

"And . . . dancing girls!" hollered the director. The spotlights snapped off, shrieks rang out, and a loud crash echoed through the room.

"Somebody get a spot on the dancing girls!"

Blue lights swung wildly around the room, first illuminating the bank of washers, then a bit of ceiling, then a row of folding chairs. Milo ducked as a light passed over the equipment cases. When he lifted his head, the light was zipping back and forth across the far wall, as if the missing dancing girls might be pinned there like museum butterflies.

It was then that a glint of silver caught Milo's eye. A pair of cages were stacked just a few ogre feet from the Office of Bragging About Stuff door. In the bottom cage, Milo was stunned to see what looked like a half dozen snoozing Tyrannosaurs. A rub of the eyes led him to reconsider this opinion and acknowledge that the creatures were simply standard-issue turkeys, albeit of dinosaurian proportion. It was a strange enough sight that Milo might have spent some time dwelling on it, had the second cage not held more worrisome contents.

Milo tugged at Tuck's sleeve.

"It disappeared," Tuck said, still staring at her ZoomBaby screen. "The dot disappeared."

"Forget the dot," said Milo, pointing to the space where the spotlight still hovered. "Look."

12

Oh, Boy

At first, Tuck looked but did not see.

Then, Milo could tell, she saw but did not believe.

Finally, when she both saw and believed, she said in a whis- per, "Oh, boy."

"Actually," said Milo, "I think that's a girl."

It was a girl, though in the time it had taken Tuck to understand what she had seen, a pair of boys had come to the front of the cage as well. They watched anxiously as their fellow

captive reached through the bars toward what Milo figured must be a latch. *Just a little farther,* he urged her silently, but it was clear even from this distance that the girl would not succeed. She and the boys were hopelessly trapped.

"We're trapped!" a chorus of voices squealed from the front of the room. The spotlight swung away from the cages and hit the screen, which retracted to reveal a quintet of shaggy ogres in sparkly gowns. They were arranged game show-esque around a sturdy marble pedestal, upon which sat an enormous, gleaming-white clothes dryer: The SuperDry 2000.

The beret whizzed through the spotlight. "You finally show up and you've got it all wrong! Mabel on the right, Eva on the left. Tanya, why are you limping?"

"I tripped over Mabel. I know you don't want us wearing them, but we can't see nothing without our glasses."

"What are we going to do?" Milo asked Tuck.

Tuck shrugged. "They'll be fine if they put their glasses back on."

"Not the chorus girls—the kids in the cage!" Milo pointed through the dark to the place where he knew the cage to be. "What are we going to do about them?"

"When Lyndon's team comes to rescue me, I'll tell them

about those kids," said Tuck. "I'm sure they'll get rescued too, if there's time."

"What if there isn't?" Milo asked. "Besides, you don't even know for sure that someone is coming."

"I saw a dot."

"What dot? Where is it now? You don't know someone is coming." Milo remembered how certain he had been that Dad was in Ogregon to complete that very rescue—and how wrong he now knew he had been. "You don't know anything," he said.

"Don't know anything? Don't know *anything*?" Tuck sputtered. "Look who's talking. Do you know how to use a ZoomBaby? Do you know about networks? About marketing? Do you know about personnel distribution? About zippers? About oaths and protocols? No. You don't know anything about anything."

Milo knew a little about networks, he thought. And who didn't know about zippers?

"You didn't even know your dad was an agent, did you, Junior Speck?"

"My name is Milo. And I know that those kids are going to get eaten if somebody doesn't do something."

"Maybe. But what are *you* going to do about it, Mi-*lo*? You don't have training. You don't have skills. You're not much bigger than an ogre spoon and, from what I can tell, not much smarter, either."

Milo reminded himself not to yell. "I was smart enough to get *somebody* out from under a bucket."

"GLASSES, SCHMASSES!" shouted the director. "You don't need to see in order to sing. MU-SIC!"

Peppy orchestral music boomed from invisible speakers. It was a snappy sort of show tune, the kind the music teacher at Milo's school liked to write new words for and have her students perform at end-of-the-year assemblies, putting aside the *"Seventy-six trombones led the big parade"* in favor of *"Seventy-four more days till we meet again."* The kind that had convinced Milo that year-round school might be okay, if only to avoid end-of-the-year assemblies.

"I'm smart enough to understand that we can't wait for someone else to help," Milo continued. "I'm smart enough to climb up to that cage and unlatch it and set those kids free."

"And *then* what are you smart enough to do? Where are you going to go after they're loose?"

"I don't know. But I'm pretty sure that being *outside* of a cage is better than being *inside* one." Milo climbed out of the cable coil.

"Wait," said Tuck.

"Wait for what? It's dark back here now . . . Everybody is watching those ogre singers—"

"Wait," said Tuck, "for me."

Milo waited as the Head of the Tuckerman Agency climbed out of the coil of cables. "It will look good in the company newsletter," she said.

Milo did not care *why* Tuck had decided to come along, but he had to admit he was glad that she had. It would be good to have someone by his side as he made the long, dark climb up those cage doors.

At the count of three, they dashed from the safety of the equipment boxes to the nearest row of folding chairs. They were far enough away from the spotlights that Milo knew they wouldn't be seen, but as he and Tuck ran from one side of the room to the other, he was still grateful for the cover the chairs provided. Finally, they reached the last chair in the row. Across an open aisle stood the towering stack of cages. Through the darkness, Milo could see the shadows of the turkeys moving restlessly behind their bars.

"You'd better hurry," whispered Tuck.

"*I'd* better?"

"Clearly, this is a one-man job. Lyndon says the Agency

manual addresses such a situation pretty straightforwardly: *Don't send two when one will do."*

A speaker crackled, the music swelled, and a sparkly ogre who was either Mabel or Eva stepped gingerly in front of the SuperDry 2000 and began to sing.

"The SuperDry 200 was a fine little dryer.
Sure, it caught fire,
and sometimes blew your houses all to bits . . ."

There was no arguing with Tuck. She wouldn't listen, and besides, she was probably right. It was a one-man—or one-kid—job. With a final glance to make sure no ogres were looking, Milo stepped out of the folding-chair tunnel and darted across the aisle.

"For months we tried to make repairs,
then came to this conclusion—
after many an explosion, concussion, and contusion—
the problem is this dryer is the pits."

The sides of the cages, Milo now saw, were solid, like the dog crates at the Downriver Pet Shop, but the doors were made of crisscrossed metal. There was enough space between crisses and crosses for Milo to find a comfortable foothold and—were he not wearing soggy slippers and continually looking over his shoulder to see if he had been spotted by a hungry ogre—would have been a cinch to climb. Even so, he made decent progress, slipping only occasionally as, hand over hand, he ascended.

"But thanks to Dr. El, things are looking swell,
and the difference is the whazzit, we can tell!
It's the whazzit makes the difference, yes, it does!
It's the whazzit makes the difference, yes, it does!"

Milo had climbed halfway up the lower cage when one of the huge, shadowy birds inside turned a watery eye upon him. It stepped closer to the bars.

Wurble, said the turkey.

"Shoo," said Milo, who, despite the limited light in the room, was noticing for the first time in his life how pointy a turkey's beak could be.

The turkey did not shoo, but moved closer.

"Vamoose," said Milo.

"Milo?" said the turkey.

Milo almost lost his grip on the bars. Did that turkey really say his name? And more importantly, did it do so in a voice he recognized? A voice he knew better than any other voice in the world?

"Dad?" said Milo.

13

The Great Escape

Milo had read a book once in which the hero's father had been captured by rats. In another, the mother had been killed by a terrible green light. He had read books in which both of the hero's parents had been made mute or uncaring or were not the people they claimed to be. But never, in all the hundreds of stories that Milo had read, had someone discovered that his father had turned into a turkey.

"How did you—" Boy and bird spoke simultaneously, a further surprise that left Milo speechless. The turkey, however, continued. "How did you get here?"

"I—I got pulled into our dryer at home, and the next thing I knew, I was here in Ogregon. Dad, what's going on?"

"Sorry, son, there isn't time to explain right now. Tell me, you're going to set those kids up there free, yes?"

Milo nodded. "Y-yes," he stammered.

"And where will you go after that?" asked the turkey. When Milo—still somewhat stunned—offered no response, the bird continued. "Listen, there's a broken elevator you can hide in. The door is stuck—it's barely open, but you can get in. When you leave this room, take a left—"

Milo found his voice. "I . . . I know," he said, recalling the OUT OF ODOR sign he had noticed on his journey into the Home Office building. "I know where it is. I've seen it."

"Good. Take those kids there and stay put."

"But what about you . . ." Milo hesitated. ". . . Dad?"

"Unlatch the turkey cage. If there's any trouble, we'll push open the door and create a diversion. Now listen, son, go straight to the elevator. Don't look back. Just run. Any questions?"

Milo had a million questions. What were they supposed to do if they were spotted in the hallway, for example? And what sort of diversion would a bunch of turkeys be able to create? And, most important of all, how did his father become poultry?

"Good, then," said Dad. "Go."

Milo peered through the shadows at the turkey's watery eye. "Can't you come with me?" he asked.

"I'm always with you," said Dad. "Now, go. We don't have much time."

It is a small word, *we*, but it can carry a lot of courage, and as soon as his father spoke it, Milo felt stronger. As quickly as he could, he shimmied across the cage door, found the latch, and lifted it from its locked position. Then he continued climbing.

Twice he lost his footing, once so completely that he slammed against the bars. *Quank*, warned the sweatshirt ducky on impact, but since the chorus ogres were still singing, nobody heard.

> *"We don't really understand it,*
> *but we're not the ones who planned it.*
> *Dr. El's the only one who has a hunch*
> *how the whazzit makes a dryer, like the SuperDry 2000,*
> *how the whazzit brings us boys for lunch!!*
> *BOYS . . . FOR . . . LUUUUUUUUNCH!!"*

When Milo finally reached the door of the second cage, the three kids inside seemed as surprised to see him as he had been to find his father transformed into a bird. One of them let out a squeal.

"*Shhhh*. Listen," Milo whispered. "I'm going to unlatch

this door, and we can all climb down. After that, you follow me, okay?"

The three kids nodded and, once the latch was opened, followed him down the cage doors as quickly as they could. Milo could not help slowing just a little as he traversed the turkey cage, in the hope that his father might speak again, but Dad did not say a word. *He's probably keeping quiet to make sure nobody overhears,* Milo told himself as his slipper finally touched the ground.

Tuck was waiting for them at the base of the cages, though if she had been impressed by Milo's actions, she didn't let on. In fact, she hardly looked up from the ZoomBaby in her hand.

"Hold it! Hold it!"

Milo spun on his heels as the ogre director's beret sailed through the spotlight.

"I can't remember the words," whined a chorus ogre.

"Not only will your duds get dry . . ." said the director wearily.

Milo sighed with relief. They hadn't been seen. Yet. "Let's go," he hissed as the chorus girl sang her line.

"Go where?" asked Tuck.

"But you'll have a tasty boy to fry and . . . Oh, dangit. Somebody get me a song sheet!"

"Someplace safe," Milo said.

The chorus ogre, having been handed a song sheet, pulled a pair of glasses from the rhinestone bosom of her costume.

Tuck looked wary. "And just how do you know—"

Milo did not want to explain about his father the turkey —besides, there wasn't time. "I just do." He waved the other kids closer, and a piercing scream filled the room.

The newly bespectacled chorus ogre scrambled over the pedestal and onto the top of the dryer. "S-s-something's moving over there!" She pointed emphatically at the turkey cage. "And it ain't just turkeys!"

"We've been spotted!" cried Milo. "Follow me!"

Spotlights swung, howls rang out, and Milo took off, sprinting out of the Office of Bragging About Stuff and down the empty hallway, the others following. Behind them, he could hear furious shouts and the panicky wurbling sound of turkeys on the loose.

"This way!" Milo panted, waving Tuck and other kids into a second corridor. "Keep going! There's an elevator on the left—the one with the OUT OF ODOR sign. Go inside. I'll be there in a minute."

The liberated girl nodded as she raced past, and the others followed her. Milo, however, could not go on without knowing. He peeked back around the corner. Several fat turkeys were hurtling out of the Bragging Office door, pursued by a pack of ogres. The turkeys darted left and right, their paths intersecting in such a way as to cause a four-ogre pileup. More ogres appeared in the doorway, and one turned to look in Milo's direction.

A sharp whistle cut through the noise. Every bird in the corridor froze, then took off running toward the opposite hall, away from the spot where Milo stood.

He felt a tug on his shirt. "Come on," said Tuck. "You're going to get us all caught."

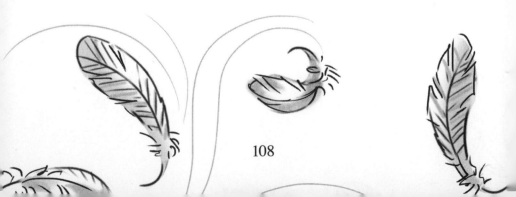

Milo took a last look down the hallway. A chorus ogre had snatched up a turkey and was squeezing it to her chest. What if that one was his dad?

Don't look back, his father had said. *Just run.*

Milo pulled his eyes away from the turkey chase and nodded. *Just run.*

14

Little Duck

The elevator had been broken for quite some time, its doors frozen in a barely open position. In willful disregard of the OUT OF ODOR sign, it gave off a significant scent of must and neglect. For the second time today, Milo was reminded of knee-deep snow as he waded through dust bunnies into the depths of the elevator.

"A-choo!" sneezed Milo.

"*Salud.*"

Milo's school had once-a-week Spanish lessons, but other than being able to use a few pleasantries and recite a list of colors, he had not learned much. Still, he tried. "*Hola,*" he said, peering through the half-dark at the cluster of formerly caged kids.

The girl rushed over, her hand raised for a high-five. "That was awesome, man! Thanks for getting us out of there!" She was still breathing hard from her run, but even in the dim light, Milo could see she was smiling. "I'm Jane."

"Milo," said Milo. "And this is—"

"Tuck," interrupted Tuck, stepping in front of Milo and extending a hand. "Head of the Tuckerman Agency." She waved the ZoomBaby as if it explained everything else. "You don't have to thank me, really. It's what I do. It's part of the Tuckerman Agency mission."

"Well, thanks for the mission! I thought we were goners." Jane shook her head. "I bet that's the fastest Little Dude has ever run." She gestured to the tiny boy who seemed unable to choose between sucking his thumb and gasping for breath. His cheeks were flushed and streaked with what Milo hoped was sweat.

"Is he okay?" Milo asked quietly.

"Ernesto thinks so. Ernesto can speak Spanish, which is what Little Dude speaks."

"He's only four," said Ernesto. "I'm eight."

"And you all came to Ogregon together?" asked Milo.

"We each got sucked into different dryers and then brought here and put in that cage together. From what I could tell, we were supposed to be part of some demonstration and—" Jane glanced cautiously at the others, then whispered. "I think those ogres were going to eat the boys."

"They'd have eaten you, too. Every human kid is a boy to them," said Tuck.

"Wow. I'm glad I didn't know that before. I guess there's a lot of stuff you guys know, with your agency and all." Jane slapped Tuck on the back. "Anyway, thanks for saving us. I'll be quiet now and you can do your thing."

Tuck looked puzzled. "My thing?"

"Sorry, I just don't know what to call it. Just, you know,

you can go ahead and get this elevator running. I can't wait to see my mom."

"¿*Mami?*" Little Dude added something else in Spanish, and Ernesto patted his hand.

"*Espera, mijo.* We'll see her soon," Ernesto said, but Little Dude sniffled anyway. "You'd better hurry. Soon as Little Dude misses his *mami,* he starts howling. Doesn't matter how far away those ogres are, they'll hear. Little Dude's got lungs."

Jane agreed. "He's, like, car-alarm-loud." They all looked at Little Dude, whose eyes were filling with tears. "You'd better get this elevator revved up."

"What?" asked Tuck.

"That's why we're in here, right? You press some buttons and it's all Willy Wonka? The magic elevator takes us home?"

Tuck looked even more confused. "I don't know about any magic elevator. I—I don't know how to get us home. This isn't my idea."

"You don't know how to get us home?" asked Ernesto.

"Then what are we doing in here?" asked Jane.

"¿*Mami?*" asked Little Dude.

"How am I supposed to know?" Tuck wheeled around to point at Milo. "Ask him. He's the one with the big ideas. 'We've got to save them,' he says. 'Run to the elevator,' he says. Ask him!"

Jane turned to Milo. "Why are we in this elevator?"

What was he supposed to say? *Because my father the turkey told me to come here?* It was the truth, but Milo didn't think it would comfort anyone. "Because it's better than being in a cage waiting to be eaten?"

For a moment Jane looked as if she might punch him, then she softened. "Yeah. I guess that's right."

"We'll be back in that cage in a minute if Little Dude goes off," said Ernesto, patting the small boy's hand.

"I'm sorry," Milo said. "I don't know what to do next. I'm not an agent. I'm just a kid." He wanted Jane and Ernesto to understand how badly he felt for getting their hopes up. He wanted Little Dude to understand too. He wished his Spanish were better, so he could explain.

"I'm sorry," he said again. *What's the word for* I? Yo, *right?* Milo squatted in front of the sniffling child. *"Yo,"* he said, clapping his hand to his chest.

Quank, said the ducky.

Little Dude stopped sniffling. *"Patito."*

"No, not *Patito.* Milo. I mean, *Yo soy Milo."* He patted his chest again. *Quank.*

Little Dude laughed. *"¡Patito!"* He said something else that Milo couldn't understand.

"Patito means 'little duck,'" explained Ernesto. "Little Dude likes your ducky."

"¡Patito, patito!" Little Dude pushed the ducky so enthusiastically that Milo lost his balance. A cloud of dust rose up around him.

Milo sneezed and got to his feet. "I'm glad you're happy, but let me *patito,* okay?" He pressed the ducky on his chest.

Quank, said the ducky. *Quank, Quank, Quank, Quank.*

"¡Ojos!" cheered Little Dude.

"He wants eggs?" asked Milo between *quanks.*

"Huevos is 'eggs,'" said Ernesto. *"Ojos* means 'eyes.' The duck's eyes spun when you fell down. He wants you to do it again."

"*¡Ojos!*" Little Dude commanded.

Milo hopped, and the ducky eyes spun. Little Dude squealed with laughter.

"*Muy bien,*" said Ernesto. "That's good. Keep going!"

Milo kept going, quanking and hopping and, occasionally, sneezing.

"I wish you did have some *huevos,*" said Jane. "We haven't had anything to eat since we got here—although I got to admit, man, the smell of you is enough to put a girl off her food. What did you do, roll around in a swamp?"

"A moldy . . . sandwich . . . actually," admitted Milo between hops. "It was kind . . . of wet, too," he said, noticing the dust that clung heavily to his corduroys.

Quank, agreed the ducky.

Just then, a shadow darkened the elevator. A large, gangly bird squeezed through the narrow entrance, its head bobbing with each stride. It was a turkey, speckled brown and ancient looking, towering Tyrannosaurus-esque above them. Milo moved in front of Little Dude, shielding him as the enormous bird moved closer.

"Dad?" asked Milo.

The turkey did not respond, but continued a few more paces, then settled into the dustiest corner of the elevator.

"Did you just call that turkey '*Dad*'?" whispered Jane.

"*¿Patito?*" asked Little Dude in a wobbly voice. His eyes were wide and worried as he stared at the turkey.

"*Muy grande patito*," said Milo. "That's all. Don't worry."

Quank, said the ducky soothingly.

Careful not to startle the enormous bird, Milo bounced just enough to goggle the sweatshirt ducky's eyes. Any second now, Jane was going to ask again, *Did you just call that turkey '*Dad*'?* He had, of course. And of course, it sounded ridiculous. It *was* ridiculous. How could his dad be a turkey? Milo must have imagined the whole thing. He must have been so scared about climbing that cage and figuring out where to hide that he went a little nuts and imagined his father's voice, as if Dad were reading him a bedtime story. Why, Milo hadn't even seen the bird's beak move, had he?

"*¡Patito!*" said Little Dude.

"Sorry," said Milo, who in his worry had ceased bouncing. He jostled himself with renewed vigor.

"*¡Patito!*"

"Little Dude," said Milo. "I'm *patito*ing . . . as much . . . as I can."

"*¡Patito! Patito!*" Little Dude pointed emphatically—but

not at the bouncing boy, nor at the ducky on his sweatshirt. Instead, the preschooler's pudgy finger pointed toward the elevator door, toward the very same spot from which a familiar voice now issued.

"Milo?"

15

Dad

"Dad?"

In the dusty shaft of hallway light stood a second turkey —darker than the first and with twice as many speckles on its wings and chest. Its neck was red and leathery, but the eye that turned toward Milo was familiar. "Dad, is that you?"

"It is," said his father's voice. "Come here, son."

Milo rushed to the turkey. "Dad!" Milo threw his arms around his father's strong, feathery drumstick.

Quank, said the ducky.

Wurble-wurble.

"Sorry," said Milo, backing up a step.

"I'm glad to see you, too, son. Do you think you can undo this?" The watery eye peered down expectantly.

Undo this? Why did people keep thinking he knew more than he did? He had no idea how his father had become a turkey, nor a single clue about how to undo whatever had been done to turn him into one. "I don't know what to do," Milo admitted.

"Just untie the knot," said his father.

In the books that Milo had read, the hero sometimes discovered a magic ring that could be twisted for wishes or a golden key that fit into a cursed lock. Perhaps there was some sort of enchanted rope somewhere that Milo would have to untangle, and when he did — *poof!* — Dad would be Dad again, and they'd all be transported home.

"In my shoelaces. Can you see it?"

Milo looked at his father's feet. Despite their considerable size, in all other ways they appeared to be regular old bird feet, knobby and scaled. They did not even have shoes on them, let alone laces.

"Lochinvar, hup!" Dad's voice rang sharply. The turkey wings lifted. "Now can you see?" Several extraordinarily long shoelaces had been knotted together and wrapped over the turkey's back and under its belly.

"*Patito!*" squeaked Little Dude.

Milo had forgotten about everyone else in the elevator. "It's okay, Little Dude. Ernesto, tell him there's nothing to worry about," he said, even though he could think of several somethings that were quite worry-worthy. For one thing, his turkey father was so tall that no matter how Milo stretched, the shoelace knots remained out of reach.

"Dad, it's a little high up."

"Hup ho," said Dad. The bird legs bent, lowering the knot into fingertip range. Milo set to work, trying to ignore the leathery head that peered impatiently over his shoulder. Instead, as his fingers fiddled, Milo stared deep into his father's dotted — or spotted — plumage. Dad's feathers were pretty, he told himself, and smooth — or at least, most of them were. One stuck out at an odd angle. It wiggled, reminding Milo of the way his father's foot tapped when he was working out a difficult problem.

"Wait a minute!" Milo abandoned the knot and grabbed hold of the wiggling dots. They did not adorn a feather at all. They adorned a sock. Which adorned a foot. Which, Milo discovered upon parting a particularly dense patch of feathers, was connected to a leg, which in turn was connected to a jacketed torso that had been lashed to the underbelly of the dinosaur-sized turkey. Milo parted the deep speckled feathers again and discovered a broad, smiling, thrillingly familiar face.

"Dad!" cheered Milo. "You're not a turkey!"

His father beamed. "Opinions differ on that account, son, but I agree with you. I am not a turkey. At the moment, however, I am rather attached to this one. How are you coming with that knot?"

The knot was now but a second's work, and soon father and son were in each other's arms.

"You were tied underneath that turkey the whole time?" asked Milo.

Dad's blue eyes sparkled. "It's an old trick—been around since Ulysses. Lashing oneself on is pretty simple, but the manual is less clear about the dismount."

"You're not supposed to talk about the manual." Out from the shadows, Tuck appeared.

"Tuck! Everyone!" said Milo. "Look! It's my dad."

"I see. Your dad is here and he's sharing classified information." Tuck pushed past Milo. "The manual is for agents only. *You're* not supposed to talk about it."

Milo's face flushed. Tuck couldn't talk to his father that

way! But before Milo could tell her so, his father spoke—calmly and with affection.

"Priscilla," said Dad. "What are you doing here?"

Priscilla?

"I go by Tuck now. It was in with your firing paperwork. And the real question is what are *you* doing here? *You* were given notice."

"End-of-the-day notice. The day wasn't over when I left Headquarters and came here. More importantly, Prisci— Tuck—there is something very wrong going on in Ogregon. There's someone here . . ." Milo's father hesitated. "There's a Dr. El—"

"I *know* about Dr. El," said Tuck. "I *am* the Head of the Tuckerman Agency."

"The Agency knows? The files were so sketchy." Dad's brow furrowed. "You've seen Dr. El?"

Tuck shrugged. "I've heard. In that room. I heard what you heard."

"Oh," said Dad. Milo could not tell if Dad looked relieved or disappointed. "There's something . . . I came here to . . ." Dad glanced at Milo. "There was something else I thought I might find."

"Excuse me?" Jane waved from her spot beside Little Dude. "I hate to interrupt, but we'd really like to get home. Can you take us home and then talk?"

Home. Of course—his father could take them home! They were all together now. There were no buckets or cages or ogres around. It was just like in a book. Milo had been brave. He had overcome obstacles. He had even helped rescue some other kids. He was kind of a hero, really. And now he'd get his reward—they'd all go home and live happily ever after.

"I'm sorry, kids," said Dad. "I can't."

Milo recognized the pained look on his father's face. It was the same one Dad wore every time Milo begged him to stay home from a business trip.

"Dad, what's the matter?"

"Just a minute, son. Tuck, did something go wrong with the oath?"

"You know I can't use the oath." Tuck kept her voice low, but Milo could still hear. "I'm not . . . Lyndon was working on getting my privileges reinstated. That's why he brought me—"

"I mean," interrupted Dad, "when you administered the oath, did something go wrong?"

Tuck blinked. "I can administer the oath?"

"It's in the manual."

"I read the manual. Some of it, anyway. It's just so big and boring and filled with stuff nobody cares about anymore. Jousting and equestrianism and falconry and fencing."

Fencing? Milo thought.

Wait a minute. *Fencing!* A thrill of realization prickled up Milo's spine.

Dad was not a door-to-door fence salesman. He was a fencing guy! A fencer! A—what was the word?—a swordsman! And his business trips? They had not been to sell chain link, but to go to places like this, like Ogregon! His father had been fighting brave battles. He had been having adventures. Milo looked with amazement at his dad. Dad looked taller somehow, his face more noble, his eyes more wise.

"Equestrianism and falconry have been pretty useful to me, eh, Lochinvar?" Milo's father patted the turkey on the flank, a gesture that seemed to Milo to be very knightly. "You might feel differently, Tuck, if you'd come to a training center."

"Lyndon says I don't need training centers." Tuck adjusted her Excellence medal. "And I don't need to read the manual, either. He's teaching me the *really* important stuff."

"Like how to fire people?" said Milo, loudly enough to startle the turkey in the dust pile.

"Easy, Gilgamesh," said Dad to the bird. "Milo, I've got this. Why don't you take a lookout post by the doors? We don't want anyone sneaking up on us."

With great reluctance, Milo did as his father asked, shuffling across the dank and dusty elevator to the narrow opening. He peered into the hallway and, finding it void of ogres, returned his attention to the conversation between his father and Tuck.

"So, Lyndon didn't teach you about swearing in emergency agents?"

Tuck shrugged. "We'd have gotten to it after all the firings were done, I'm sure."

Puffs of dust rose as Dad's foot tapped. "You're Head of the Tuckerman Agency now, Tuck. You may have lost some of your personal privileges, but lineage law makes you the ranking Tuckerman. You—and only you—have the power to use the oath to swear in emergency agents. Whoever you swear in will then have the ability to zip everybody else back to Headquarters."

"What?" said Milo. "Are you saying we could have gone home all along?"

Tuck waved the ZoomBaby at the kids around her. "They don't have any training."

"You don't need training to become a Tuckerman Agent, only to become a good one," said Dad. "Generations of Agency heads have deputized in emergencies. Your father did it during the Chupacabra Crisis. Administer the oath, Tuck. Let your emergency agent take you all home. Then, when you're all safely at Headquarters, you can fire whoever you've deputized. You know you have *that* power."

"Excuse me again," said Jane. "But could somebody just tell me if we are going home?"

"*Mami?*" sniffed Little Dude.

"I'm sorry, kids," said Milo's father. "We'll get you home, but we'll need one of you to help us out."

"I'll do it." Jane stepped forward. "If it'll get us home, I'll do it."

Dad smiled his approval, and Milo felt a twist of jealousy. He hurried back to his father's side. "I'll do it too."

"Thank you, son, but we'll only need one volunteer," said Dad. "No sense getting you any more entangled in this than you already are."

Milo nodded and tried to smile. They were going to be okay, after all. Jane was going to get them home. And yet, Milo could not help but wish that *he* was the one becoming an agent and taking them to safety.

Wurble-wurble! The turkeys swung their heads toward the hallway.

"Shut up, birds," said Tuck.

"They have names," said Milo.

"Shhhhh!" said Milo's father. "Listen."

Shouting could be heard in the distance. "Tuckerman has escaped! Tuckerman has escaped!"

Milo made for his lookout position, but Dad grabbed his arm. "Wait. There's not much time. Tuck is going to swear in—"

"Jane," said Jane.

"And then you kids can zip out of here. I'll catch up with you soon."

"You're not coming with us?" cried Milo.

"You heard me earlier, son. I can't go back yet."

"I thought you couldn't *take* us back. Because you were fired."

"I can return home from this mission, and I will, but then my days as an agent will be over. Before I leave, I've got to learn more about what's going on here, about this Dr. El. I've got to see that dryer in action—"

"You're going back to that room full of ogres? You can't! They'll catch you! They'll—" A loud rumbling stopped Milo midsentence.

"Kids! Against the doors," commanded Dad.

They all did as his father commanded, pressing themselves against the elevator doors and out of sight.

"Check outside, then come back!" snarled a voice Milo recognized. It was Roger, the singing security ogre. "I'll start with the offices."

Footsteps thudded and doorknobs rattled. Twice, Milo heard hinges creak and voices grumble. The sounds came closer. Dad clucked his tongue, and the two turkeys rose from their spots in the dust to stand in front of Milo and the other kids. Milo held his nose to keep from sneezing. He peered through Gilgamesh's tail feathers just in time to see a flashlight poke between the elevator doors. A beam of light swept along the dusty back wall, and the rest of the elevator darkened as the security ogre pressed his face against the narrow opening to peek inside.

"Got anything?" called a voice in the hallway.

The flashlight beam traversed the far wall, the floor, the ceiling. Then it clicked off. "All clear. I told Captain Magnesson ain't no way them wimpy legs could carry Tuckerman this far. He's hiding in that supply closet someplace, I know it."

"We'll search it again. But I'm telling you, if I find any boys in there, I'm eating 'em. I don't care what our orders is."

The sound of ogre footsteps receded, and Dad peeked outside. "I've got to go now,

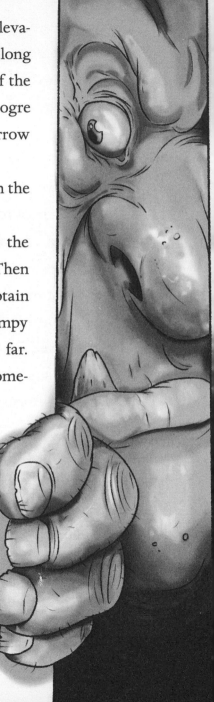

before any other patrols come by. Lochinvar! *Chirrup!*" The turkey rose to its feet, and Milo's dad was swiftly beside it. "Give Jane the oath, Tuck, and go back to Headquarters."

"But, Dad," cried Milo, "Tuck fired you! You can come home. This isn't your job anymore."

"Just because it's not my job, son, doesn't mean it's not my responsibility." Dad checked his watch. "It's two thirty now. The demo starts at five, and once those Big Wigs discover there's no one left to Squash, it won't last long. I'll meet you all at Headquarters in about three hours." Milo's father gave him another strong hug. "I wouldn't be doing this if it wasn't important, son. I've got to find out all I can about Dr. El. Go home. Be safe."

With a kiss on the head, Dad broke away from his son. "Plotz," he said, and the turkey sat. He stepped up onto the bird's speckled wing and swung gracefully onto its back. With a low *chirrup,* Lochinvar rose.

He was leaving. His father was really leaving. "Let me come with you," said Milo.

"You're always with me," said Dad. Then he and his speckled steed squeezed through the elevator opening and dashed away.

16

I Swear

For a moment, things had been almost exactly as Milo had wished when he had been sock sorting earlier that day. The two of them, father and son, about to head home from an adventure. But now Dad was gone and once again Milo had been left behind, stuck in a dusty and odorous elevator listening to some other kid get sworn in as a Tuckerman Agent.

"Ernesto? Little Dude? You shall be witnesses." Tuck's voice took on a formal air as she turned to face Jane. "I shall say the Tuckerman oath and then you shall repeat it. Are you prepared?"

"I'm prepared," said Jane, matching Tuck's tone of solemnity.

Milo pushed his slipper against the filthy floor. Dust rose, clouding the scene before him.

"Hey, Junior Speck, could you cut it out?" said Tuck.

"We're doing a ceremony over here." Right hand raised, she turned back to Jane and recited the oath, which Jane, with great dignity, repeated.

"I swear as a Tuckerman Agent to do my duty with courage and wisdom and utmost fidelity, until all that can be done has been done."

"When I was named an agent, my father used a sword, but this will have to do." Tuck tapped the ZoomBaby on Jane's shoulders. "Arise and take up your responsibility."

"Arise?" asked Jane.

Tuck scowled. "Shoot. You were supposed to kneel. I don't think it will matter, though."

"Guess we'll find out," said Milo. His voice sounded bitter, even to him.

"Once a person is an agent," continued Tuck, "she can zip out of a place whenever she needs to by repeating the oath and declaring a mission. That's the tricky part."

"It doesn't sound tricky," said Milo.

"Shows what you know," said Tuck. "In the old days, agents used to declare these crazy missions like 'Retrieve the Holy Grail' or 'Rescue every fair damsel in the land,' and then they'd be stuck."

Jane gave Tuck a wary look. "Why?"

"*Every* fair damsel? Get real. Agents would either be killed in the attempt or stay where they were forever because their pride wouldn't let them break the oath — 'What can be done has been done' and all that. If an agent returned without completing his mission, he'd lose his privileges forever. That was before we had a reinstatement board. It's hard to get your privileges back now, but then it was impossible."

"I just want to get us all out of here," said Jane. "I say the oath again, right?" Jane cleared her throat. "I swear as a Tuckerman Agent to do my duty with courage and . . ."

"And wisdom," reminded Tuck.

". . . and wisdom and utmost fidelity, until all that can be done has been done. Now what?"

The *what* was soon obvious. A strand of silver light appeared, stretching from the floor to a spot above Jane's head. At first, the light was no more than a thread, but as it grew thicker, sharp horizontal ridges emerged on its surface. A shiny silver ring dangled from the very top.

"It looks like a zipper," said Milo.

"Didn't you hear your dad?" said Tuck. "We're going to zip back to Headquarters. Go ahead, Jane. Open it."

The newly sworn-in agent reached up for the silver ring

and pulled it smoothly down to the floor. As she did, the zipper's teeth separated and a hazy light appeared in the opening. Beyond it, Milo could make out a spacious wood-paneled room with a high ceiling and several desks. On the back wall hung a painting of an armor-clad knight who appeared to be holding a sewing-needle sword and a four-holed button as a shield.

"We go in there?" Jane asked.

Tuck nodded. "Tuckerman Agency Headquarters. There's nobody around right now. Lyndon gave everyone who wasn't in the field the Thanksgiving holiday off. Anyway, state your mission, and then we can go through. Be quick. The zipper doesn't stay open long."

Jane tugged at one side of the zipper. The air around it rippled, as if a curtain were being pulled back from a window.

"State your mission," said Tuck.

"My mission is to get us all out of Ogregon." Jane pulled the zipper wide and extended her leg into the space. It took on a fuzzy quality, like bad television reception.

"Whoa! I'm fizzy!"

"You'll solidify once you're all the way in," Tuck assured her.

And that is what happened. As Jane stepped through the zipper, her entire body fizzed like freshly poured ginger ale. For a moment, she was little more than a golden ghost. Then, as she moved deeper into the paneled room, she grew solid again. She turned and waved. "It's fine, Ernesto. C'mon, Little Dude!"

Milo watched as Ernesto took Little Dude's hand and they stepped through the effervescent light and into the Tuckerman Agency office.

"¡Que chido!" Ernesto gave Jane a high-five. "That was awesome!"

"¡Patito!" squealed Little Dude.

"I'm coming," said Milo.

"¡Patito!" Little Dude said again, tears filling his eyes. He said something else to Ernesto and waved a finger not at Milo, but at the turkey nesting in the dust.

"He doesn't want to leave the bird behind," Ernesto translated.

Milo turned to Gilgamesh. It might not be as good as becoming a Tuckerman Agent, but he could still contribute something. He could save this giant bird for Little Dude.

"Will it fit through the zipper?" he asked Tuck.

"The space stretches," said Tuck. "But we don't have time—"

Milo was already at the turkey's side. "Come on, Gilgamesh," he said. "Let's go."

The turkey did not budge.

Milo ran behind the bird and pushed against its tail feathers. "Giddyup!" he said. Gilgamesh neither giddied nor upped. Tuck, however, guffawed.

"You think you're so smart?" said Milo from behind the bird. "You try it."

The Head of the Tuckerman Agency clapped her hands. "Come," she said, as if calling a naughty spaniel.

Wurble, said Gilgamesh, though he did not move.

"I said, *come!*" Tuck commanded, twice as loudly.

The turkey scrambled backwards, pinning Milo to the wall. "You're scaring him!" called Milo through feathers.

"Hey, bird!" Tuck flapped her arms, running full-speed toward the cornered turkey. "Get moving!"

Gilgamesh, who was not used to being addressed in such a manner, flapped as well and darted away.

"¡Patito!" called Little Dude.

Milo turned toward the voice — and the zipper. "It's closing! Tuck! Run!" he yelled, but before either could move, the ring reached its apex and the silver light dissolved.

"We missed it," said Milo, staring at the space where the zipper had once been.

Tuck shrugged. "It's just as well. Saves me the firing paperwork."

"What do you mean?"

"She didn't complete her mission, did she? She was supposed to get *all* of us out of Ogregon and she failed. Poof! No more zipper privileges."

"That wasn't her fault," said Milo. "It was yours."

"Mine? *I* wasn't the one trying to rescue a stupid turkey."

"*I* wasn't the one scaring it!"

"Well, you're scaring it now!"

Poor Gilgamesh was frantic with fear. Dust swirled as

the bird flapped anxiously; its long, leathery neck stretched, its watery eye wild.

"Oh, hey," said Milo softly. "I'm sorry, fella. Sorry, Gilgamesh. I didn't mean to scare you."

The turkey stopped flapping.

"It's okay." Milo took a small step toward the bird, his hand outstretched. The bird sat. "You're a good turkey. Everything's going to be fine." Slowly, Milo moved closer and closer, until he was near enough to stroke Gilgamesh's soft, feathery chest. "That's it. You're okay."

"Of course. You're a freaking bird whisperer," said Tuck. "Must run in the family."

Milo could only smile. "Dad did seem pretty good with them." He patted Gilgamesh as he had seen his father do.

"Not your dad, dope. Your mother."

"My mother?" said Milo, loud enough to startle the bird. "Sorry, pal." He forced himself to speak slowly and calmly, though he was experiencing neither state. "You know my mom?"

"Duh," said Tuck, in a not very Head-of-the-Tuckerman-Agency way. "Your mother

is Eleanor Speck, right? Lyndon said she's the one with the animal skills. Pretty good at tech, too, I hear."

"My mother is a Tuckerman Agent?" said Milo.

"You really don't know anything, do you? Tell me, Junior Speck, why do you think your dad's never home?"

"Business trips," said Milo, though his image of what his father did on those trips was now quite different than it had been just a few hours ago. "Your agency sent him on missions, I mean."

"Your dad? On Agency missions? Your dad's just a trainer —that's why he was in the Fencing Office." The superior tone had returned to Tuck's voice. "The Agency did not *send* your dad on missions, he went on his own. Lyndon discovered it during a zipper audit. It's one of the reasons we fired him."

Milo thought about all those weekends he had spent alone with Grandmother, repairing blenders and sorting socks, wishing his father were by his side. "Are you saying Dad went away voluntarily? That he could have been home with me all the time?"

"He could have," said Tuck, "if he weren't always out searching for your mother. Anyway, now that you've calmed down Googlehead—"

"Gilgamesh," said Milo, though his reply came from the same automatic part of his brain that spent the majority of its workday keeping his heart beating and his lungs pumping. The rest of his brain was trying to recover from the impact of the information that Tuck had just slammed into it.

His father—who was not a door-to-door fence salesman, but a trainer for some mysterious secret agency—had spent the last year searching for Mom. And she—Milo's mother—was a part of this agency too. She hadn't left Milo to "get away from it all." She had been on a Tuckerman Agency mission and gotten lost or hurt or something. At least, that's what his father must believe if he had spent so much time searching for her.

Milo shook his head. It was more than he could make sense of, really. If brains had necks, his would have whiplash.

"Hey. Junior Speck." Tuck snapped her fingers. "I'm talking to you."

"You are?"

"Yeah. I said kneel down and I'll make you an agent so you can zip us out of here."

"Oh, okay. Sure." Milo kneeled on the lint-covered carpet.

"Raise your right hand," said Tuck.

Milo followed instructions, raising his hand and repeating the oath. Tuck tapped his shoulders with her ZoomBaby.

"Now, say the oath again and call the zipper—and declare a really big mission, will you? One you know you can't do? That way I won't have to fill out any of the firing paperwork. It took, like, two days to get your dad's papers in order. Total nightmare."

Tuck went on talking about forms and filing, but Milo had stopped listening. He was a Tuckerman Agent now. A Tuckerman Agent. Just like his dad—and his mom. Except, of course, that he was sitting here safe in a dusty elevator while Dad was risking his life to stop a bunch of hungry ogres from turning human kids into snack food, and Mom was . . . Well, he didn't know what his mom was doing, but chances were she was doing something important and brave too. Or she was trapped. Or hurt. Or lost.

And Dad was giving up his last chance to find her so he could learn more about this Dr. El guy and help save other kids from being sucked into Ogregon and eaten. Kids he didn't even know.

That's what Dad had said, wasn't it? He could only call the zipper once more, and then that was it? He would go home and his firing would take effect and he wouldn't be an agent anymore?

It didn't seem fair. It wasn't like his father was sitting around doing nothing. He shouldn't have to give up his last chance to find—

"Speck? Speck?" Tuck was snapping again. "Are you listening to me?"

Milo nodded, though he had not been. Nor was he listening now. Not to Tuck, anyway. Instead, he was straining to hear the tiny voice of an idea that was forming inside him.

"That zipper . . ." said Milo. "An agent can call it at any time?"

"As soon as he's sworn in, yeah. So, get to it."

"Or," said Milo, the idea growing louder, "not."

17

Shall We Dance?

"Not?" said Tuck. *"Not?* An hour ago you dragged me out of that supply closet—from which I am certain Lyndon was about to rescue me—all panicky about not waiting around, and now, when you have the power to take us to Headquarters right away, you say *not?"*

The small idea that had begun to form just seconds ago was growing louder, but Milo had not yet made sense of it. He stalled for time, babbling the first words that came to him. "I . . . I just want to be here while my dad is in danger. I know I can't help him. But, I just want . . . you know?"

"Of course I know," said Tuck. A wave of hair fell over one of her eyes, but she didn't brush it away. "Look. If Lyndon hadn't sent out a team of investigators, I never would have known what happened to my father. Sometimes I think if I'd been there, maybe he'd have zipped back home with me instead of fighting. Maybe he'd have seen me and thought there was something more important . . . Never mind. Never mind what I said. It's classified." Tuck tapped on her ZoomBaby. "Okay, Junior Speck. We'll wait a little while. Jane and those boys can hang out by themselves for a bit, I guess. But you have to promise me that you will call the zipper at the first sign of trouble."

"First sign," Milo promised.

Wurble-wurble, said Gilgamesh.

Tuck went off to a dusty corner, the light of her ZoomBaby shining on her face. Milo had made her sad, and he was sorry about it, but he couldn't dwell on that right now. Instead, he turned his thoughts to his idea.

In the last few seconds, it had become completely clear to him. He needed to be a Tuckerman Agent. One who wouldn't declare too big a mission or make Tuck decide to fire him. A real permanent agent, with the power to zip around wherever he wanted. Then he and Dad could look for Mom together.

All he needed to do was convince Tuck. But how? He didn't even know what an agent did, really. An image of his father, strong and sure, filled Milo's mind. He had seen the way Dad commanded those turkeys, the ease with which he had swung himself up onto Lochinvar's back. How tall he had sat, how impressive he had sounded.

"Chirrup!" Milo said, remembering his father's command. Instantly, the bird beside him stood, its head angled as if waiting for further orders. "Whoa! Tuck, did you see that?"

Tuck pretended she had not.

"What else can you do?" he asked Gilgamesh. "Can you sit?" Milo demonstrated. "Like this. Sit." What had Dad said? "Plotz!" The turkey ruffled its speckled feathers, then settled back into the dust pile.

"Cool!" said Milo. "Okay, um, chirrup again!" Gilgamesh stood. "What about this? What about walking? Walk!" Milo marched in place, and Gilgamesh mimicked him, pacing in time with Milo's steps.

"You two make lovely dance partners," said Tuck.

"We do, don't we? Gilgamesh, dance!" said Milo, and he began directing the enormous bird in the only dance he knew.

"First you wiggle and you wiggle," sang Milo, shaking his hips from side to side. After a moment's pause, Gilgamesh shook his tail feathers.

"Yes!" cheered Milo. *"Then you flap your little wings."* Milo flapped. Gilgamesh did the same.

"Then go like this." Milo made beaks of his hands and thrust them forward in time with his song. Gilgamesh only stared.

"Are you teaching that turkey to chicken dance?" asked Tuck.

"Yes, yes, yes, yes," Milo sang as he clapped. *"Then you wiggle and you wiggle, then you flap and you flap, then go like this."* Again, Gilgamesh wiggled and flapped, but only looked confused during the beak part.

"It doesn't have hands, you know. You should have it move its feet instead. Like you did before." Tuck stood up, dropping her ZoomBaby into her jacket pocket. She marched in place for a moment, then made her way over to Gilgamesh. *"First you wiggle and you wiggle, then you flap and you flap, then stomp your feet,"* she sang as she danced. Clouds of dust rose, but the turkey followed every gesture and step.

Milo sneezed, then joined in. *"First you wiggle and you wiggle, then you flap and you flap, then stomp your feet."*

Clap! Clap! Clap! Clap!

"This is really kind of cool," sang Tuck as they wiggled.

"Yes, it's really kind of cool," sang Milo as they flapped.

"Oh, yes, it is," they sang together as they stomped.

Clap! Clap! Clap! Clap!

They sang and danced through several more verses, making up lyrics as they went.

"That turkey's listening to me," sang Tuck at Milo.

"I wish my dad were here to see," sang Milo at Tuck.

Tuck stopped singing. "I'm sure you do. Dance on, Junior Speck. I got stuff to do." She pulled her ZoomBaby out of her pocket and headed back to her spot on the floor.

"Hey, I shouldn't have brought up—"

Tuck held up her hand. "Shhh . . . working," she said. "Classified."

Gilgamesh, too, was done with dancing. He had returned to his dust pile and appeared to be napping.

Milo had kind of screwed up, mentioning his dad, but before that, he and Tuck had been getting along. That had to be good. Still, Milo was pretty sure he was a long way from convincing her to let him remain an agent. What he really needed to do, he thought, was something that would prove his worth. But what?

"I just want to help my dad, I just want to help my dad," Milo sang under his breath. *"And find my mom."*

It was not quite under enough.

"Could you find another song?" asked Tuck. "That one's getting annoying."

"Sorry." Milo tried to shake the chicken dance from his head. The only other tune that came to mind was the one the ogre showgirls had been rehearsing.

"Thanks to Dr. El, things are looking swell.
It's the whazzit makes the difference, yes, it does!
It's the whazzit makes the difference, yes, it does!"

Milo pictured the whazzit he had seen on the Bragging Office screen. Its wedge shape. The small hinges at its sides. The tiny hooks on the—

"That's it!" said Milo.

"What's it?" asked Tuck.

"Exactly."

It should be noted that although Milo was a clever boy with a good mind for fixing things, he had no idea how ogre dryers transported human children from one world to another. Just as with the Tuckerman Agency zippers, he guessed there was some weird combination of physics and magic involved, but he could not claim to understand it.

He did, however, understand the mechanics of the dryer itself. He knew how the parts fit together to make a machine that would use motion, heat, and air to dry clothing. Studying the diagram in the repairman's truck had given him a basic understanding of the SuperDry 200 as well, including the loose-fitting parts and shoddy workmanship that made it so dangerous to use. Even back when he was bouncing around on the moldy sandwich and trying not to think about being eaten, it had seemed likely to him that the space in front of the lint trap was too large and was the reason for the dryer's frequent fires and explosions. Now he was sure of it.

"The whazzit," Milo said. "It's the whazzit makes the difference."

"I heard you the first time," said Tuck. "Can you sing something else? 'The Yellow Rose of Texas,' maybe? Or 'Yankee Doodle'?"

"Not the song, the whazzit itself. Listen. There's something about that clothes dryer that transports kids to Ogregon. I don't think the ogres understand how it works—"

150

"No surprise there," said Tuck.

"Yeah, well, I don't understand how that part works either, but I think I know why it doesn't happen very often. Look." Milo waved Tuck closer to the elevator wall. Trailing his finger through the grimy dust, he drew a simple plan of the SuperDry 200, explaining how lint and bits of debris clogged the air vent and caught on fire. "I think most of the time those explosions happen before any kids can get sucked up out of our world and brought to Ogregon."

"Uh-huh," said Tuck. "And the whazzit stops that?"

"The whazzit fits perfectly in front of the lint trap, see? And when the hinge part flips open, these little hooks keep it in place." Milo drew the open hinge with its clawlike hooks grabbing hold just under the lint screen. "The whazzit directs the airflow, so that all that stuff gets caught in the trap like it's supposed to. Nothing sucks up underneath it. Nothing clogs the air vent. Nothing catches on fire, so no explosion."

"And if there's no explosions . . ." said Tuck.

"Then every time an ogre does a load of laundry, he'll also get a kid."

"Well. You've got it all figured out, don't you, Junior Speck? Fine. You're a bird whisperer *and* a mechanical genius," said Tuck. "Now, *I've* got an idea. Let's call the zipper, go back to Headquarters, and tell somebody who can do something about it. Remember, I don't want to do the paperwork, so you just declare a super-big mission, okay?"

"No!" said Milo. He tried to sound casual. "I mean, of course we could zip back. I'm just surprised you'd want to. I mean, I thought you were trying to impress that Lyndon guy and get your privileges back. But if you don't care about that—"

"Of course I care about that," snapped Tuck.

"Well, that Dr. El is going to show off the whazzit in, like, two hours, right?"

Tuck tapped her ZoomBaby. "One hour and fifty-five minutes."

He was running out of time. Milo spoke faster. "Okay. So, you don't know how long it will take to get back to Headquarters and round up all your agents and fill them in on all the details and send them back here, do you? They're on Thanksgiving holiday, right? It could take a long time, right?"

"It could," admitted Tuck.

"And the whole time, Dr. El could be using the whazzit and catching kids and maybe even eating them on live TV, right?"

"Yeah, I guess."

"But what if there was already someone here in Ogregon—like, maybe, the Head of the Tuckerman Agency—who could save the day?" said Milo. "Seems pretty impressive to me."

"I guess so." Tuck seemed to be considering Milo's idea. "But what could I do? I'm sort of small by ogre standards, you know. And you? You're positively minuscule."

"Sometimes small is an advantage. Look. We can . . . um . . . we could crawl in here." He pointed to an open space he had drawn at the back of the dryer. "And then make our way through the machine to where the lint trap is. After that, all we have to do is block the whazzit hinge from opening all the way."

"We just stand there and block the whazzit from working? For how long? Won't it get hot? Won't we explode?"

Oh, yeah, thought Milo, though he did not say it aloud. "Um . . . no. We wouldn't just stand there. We'd jam the space with something. Block the hinge so it couldn't open."

"Block it with what?" said Tuck, looking around the elevator. "There's nothing here but dust bunnies and an oversized pigeon."

Wurble-wurble, said Gilgamesh.

Milo stared at the diagram he had drawn in the dust. What could they find that would fit the space? "Well, just about anything would work, so long as it stopped the whazzit from opening all the way. A pencil might work."

Did he just say a pencil? Well, sure. Why not? A pencil. A pencil might be thick enough do the trick. He looked at the space again. "Maybe two or three pencils bundled together?"

Tuck pretended to search the elevator again. "Sorry. No pencils in here."

"This hallway is filled with offices," said Milo. "All we have to do is find an open door. What office doesn't have pencils?"

Tuck did not look convinced. "Let's pretend your plan works and the dryer explodes with the whazzit inside. So what? Can't they just build another whazzit?"

"Maybe. I don't know." Milo thought back to what he had heard in the Bragging Office. "But that director lady said this whazzit was the only one in existence. If we blow it up, then you'll have time to go back to your Headquarters and get a whole division of agents before they can make another. It would be a brave and noble thing, wouldn't it? Blowing up the whazzit and then returning to Headquarters with vital information? Exactly the sort of thing that would get your privileges back? That would impress Lyndon?"

"Well . . ." said Tuck.

"Plus, we've got a foolproof escape route. I promise to call the zipper at the first sign of trouble."

"You already promised that."

"I double promise." Milo raised his right hand, just as he had to take the Tuckerman Oath.

"Fine." Tuck checked her ZoomBaby. "But if we're going to do this thing, we'd better hurry."

"That's where he comes in." Milo gestured toward Gilgamesh. "Give me your shoelaces."

"Nuh-uh," said Tuck. "I am not hanging upside down under a turkey."

"You're not going to hang upside down. Just give me your shoelaces."

Tuck unlaced her shoes. Then she pulled several matching pairs of laces from her jacket pocket. "An agent carries spares. It's surprising how something as small as a broken shoelace can mess up a mission."

Milo tied the laces into one long rope with a slipknot at one end. "Easy, boy." He stepped slowly toward the spot where the turkey sat. "I'm just going to slide this over your head."

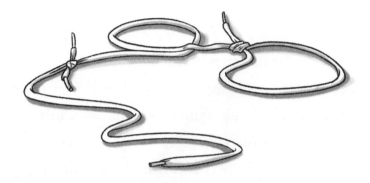

The task was simpler than Milo had expected, as the great bird seemed to understand what was needed. He lowered his head, and Milo slipped the shoelace loop over it. Climbing onto Gilgamesh's back, however, proved much more difficult, and it took several tries before Milo was able to find a foothold on the turkey's wing and heave himself into position. Once there, he took hold of the shoelace with one hand and helped Tuck up with the other. Soon both were settled, Tuck behind Milo on Gilgamesh's broad, bony back, their legs tucked neatly under his wings.

"Ready?" asked Milo.

"Just a sec." Tuck pulled her ZoomBaby out of her pocket and held it at arm's length behind her. "Duck down, Junior Speck. I want to get a picture of me on Gargantuan."

"It's Gilgamesh," said Milo.

"Whatever. You're blocking the view of its head."

Milo ducked, and Tuck snapped a photo.

"Alert. Low Battery," said the ZoomBaby.

Tuck turned off the device and dropped it into her pocket. "Better save the battery. I'll probably want some shots of me in action later. Okay, Junior Speck. Let's go."

Milo gave the shoelace rein a small tug. "Chirrup," he said, and the turkey rose to its feet. The riders wobbled and wavered, but managed to stay astride.

"Okay. Good boy. Now let's try walking. Ready? Walk." At Milo's command, Gilgamesh staggered forward. It was not a smooth ride, but after a few practice laps around the elevator, Milo worried less that he and Tuck would fall to their deaths. He tugged the shoelace to the right, and the bird stepped cautiously toward the elevator door.

"Whoa," said Milo as they reached the narrow opening. Gilgamesh froze. "Good bird." He stroked the turkey's feathers and listened intently for ogre activity. All was silent.

Milo remembered how Dad had looked when he left for

the Office of Bragging About Stuff with Lochinvar. Tall and brave and strong.

Milo sat straighter. "Let's go," he said. And with a flick of the shoelace, the two riders and their noble steed squeezed out of the darkened elevator and into the corridor beyond.

18

The First Sign of Trouble

"Which way?" whispered Tuck.

The two riders and their feathered steed had emerged from the elevator and stood now in the long Home Office home office hallway. To the right, Milo knew, the corridor intersected with one that led to the Office of Bragging About Stuff, which was certain to be filled with busy ogres. "Left," said Milo. He tugged on the shoelace reins, and they started down the dimly lit hall.

In the books that Milo had read, now would be the time when the hero would come upon a door that had been propped open for one reason or another, and he would lead his party quickly inside to safety. Every door in the Home Office home office hallway, however, was shut tight.

"Figures," said Milo.

"Call the zipper," said Tuck.

"I said I'd call at the first sign of trouble. This is not trouble. This is inconvenience."

Milo surveyed the two doors closest to them. OFFICE OF SHAVING TECHNOLOGY, read one. OFFICE OF KITCHEN STUFF, read the other. The Kitchen Stuff door had been open when Milo had first traveled this hallway, and he remembered seeing a lab-coated ogre assaulting a toaster inside. From his position astride Gilgamesh, he could not see through the frosted glass to be certain the ogre was gone, but he did see that the two lights dangling from the ceiling were dark.

Milo guided Gilgamesh closer to the Kitchen Stuff door until the bird was leaning against it. "Push," said Milo. Gilgamesh pushed, but the door did not open. "We're going to have to turn the knob."

"Yeah, right," said Tuck, for despite their elevated status atop Gilgamesh, the doorknob was clearly out of reach. "Call the zipper."

Milo did not want to call the zipper. "Maybe you could reach it if you stood on my shoulders."

"Get lost," said Tuck.

"Come on. I'll hold on to your feet. You won't fall. And think of how brave you'll sound when you tell this part of the story to Lyndon."

160

Milo heard a sigh and felt a jostling behind him. First one shoe, then another, settled heavily on his shoulders. Milo held them tight and tried to keep steady. "You can do this," he said.

"Ha!" said Tuck, "I already did!"

Milo peeked up. Tuck was hugging the doorknob, her smile reflecting in its shiny surface. "Can you turn it?" he asked.

Tuck twisted. The door flew open and Tuck flew with it, for although her grip was tight on the doorknob and Milo's grip was tight on her shoes, there were no shoelaces to keep the Head of the Tuckerman Agency's shoes gripping tightly to her feet. Instead, those feet pedaled wildly in the air as the stranded girl clung desperately to the Office of Kitchen Stuff doorknob.

"Hold on!" called Milo.

"What a good idea," Tuck gasped. "Another brilliant plan from Junior Speck!"

Milo tucked the girl's empty shoes under his arm and steered Gilgamesh to a spot beneath her. "Steady, buddy," he said in a slow, calm voice. "Steady . . . Stay . . . Tuck, can you—" The rest of his sentence proved unnecessary, as Tuck had already found her footing upon Milo's shoulders and was stepping back down onto the turkey's bony back.

"You okay?" asked Milo, handing Tuck her shoes.

"Oh, I'm just aces." Tuck spoke with less sarcasm than Milo would have expected. "Let's get your pencils."

Milo nodded and surveyed the room. It was filled with mixers and blenders and can openers and coffeemakers, all of which seemed to have suffered fates equal to or worse than the toaster he had seen hurled across the room earlier that afternoon. Broken gadgetry littered the floor, and many of the appliances were scorched and blackened. The room was cluttered and chaotic, but blissfully devoid of ogres.

"Watch your step," Milo whispered as he urged Gilgamesh forward. Gilgamesh took three quiet steps, and the office door slammed closed behind them.

Bellowing erupted in the corridor. "Down there! One of the offices!"

"We've got to hide!" said Milo frantically.

"We've got to call the zipper!" said Tuck, matching Milo's tone exactly.

Had Gilgamesh been able to speak a language understandable to either, he might have said "We've got to get out of here!" But since he could not, and since, like most birds, he held the philosophy that actions spoke louder than words, he bolted into a run, neck stretched, wings flared, clawed feet finding little traction on the slippery office floor. He circled the office's central worktable, tripping on coils and metal bits as he skittered and veered. Milo clung desperately to the shoelace reins. Tuck clung desperately to Milo. *Quank,* yelped the sweatshirt ducky with every step. *Quank, Quank, Quank, Quank, Quank!*

Gilgamesh skidded around another corner. A pyramid of broken toasters blocked their path.

"Look out!" cried Milo.

"I'll take Shaving," hollered a voice in the hallway. "You look in Kitchen Stuff!"

The turkey's feet seemed to slip out from under him. This was it, Milo knew. They were going to crash. They were going to be discovered.

"Call the zipper!" urged Tuck.

"Right! Okay!" said Milo. "I vow — whoa!"

Suddenly they were flying, the great bird flapping and soaring toward the ceiling, then landing on the rim of the bowl-like light fixture, which swung pendulum-esque under their weight. Gilgamesh slipped into the concave shade, settling down as if to roost.

"Wow," said Milo. "Did you know turkeys could do that?"

"Shhh!" Tuck pointed at the frosted window in the Kitchen Stuff door and the silhouette of the shaggy ogre just beyond it.

The lamp ceased swinging as the office door crashed open. A hulking security ogre thundered inside.

"You in here, Tuckerman?" he said, kicking aside a waffle iron. It was Roger, sounding angrier and more desperate than ever. "You know, you got me in a lot of trouble, escaping from the bucket like that. Well, fool me once, shame on you. Fool me twice, I eat you with barbeque sauce."

"Call the zipper," Tuck whispered. "Call it now!"

Milo shook his head. Roger was rounding the worktable. Milo did not dare whisper the oath, nor call that silvery light. What if the ogre heard them before they had a chance to open the zipper and step through?

"Come out, come out, wherever you are!" The security ogre stomped through the toaster pile. "Oh, I know. You'll like this one, Tuckerman. Ready? Fee-fi-fo-fum." He was just below them now, directly under their lampshade hiding

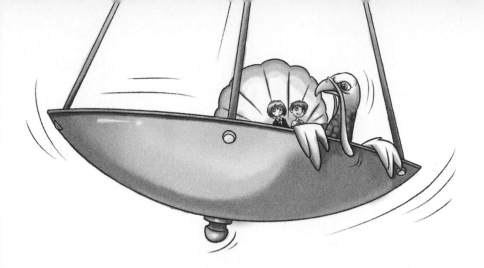

spot. "I smell the blood of an Englishman!" The ogre snick-
ered. Then, playing his part to the fullest, he took a huge
sniff. "Hey . . ." He sniffed again. "I *do* smell something . . ."

"The oath," Tuck whispered again. "Say the—"

"I smell," Roger muttered, sniffing a third time, "turkey
sandwich."

19

Springing into Action

Milo felt Tuck poke him hard in the ribs. It was true, he still smelled like rancid sandwich. The security ogre had to have caught a whiff of *him*.

Roger rifled through the piles on the worktable, overturning a toolbox and scattering its contents. "A sandwich would be pretty nice, I'll tell you that much, Tuckerman. Nobody remembers that security guys need breaks too. It's just, 'Don't leave your post, Roger.' 'How could you be fooled by a tape recorder, Roger?' Don't nobody say, 'Howdja you like a McGobbler's MegaMeal, Roger?' or 'Talented guy like you deserves a bite of boy.'"

"Who you talking to?" A second security ogre appeared in the doorway.

"Nobody," said Roger. "I thought I smelled something."

"Tuckerman?"

"A sandwich."

"A sandwich would be good. Nobody remembers that security guys need breaks too."

"That's what I'm saying." Roger slapped the worktable in agreement, and a nearby shelf collapsed, sending a half dozen slow cookers crashing to the floor. "Whoopsie."

"Don't worry about it. Listen, them Big Wigs are already showing up for the demo, and catering will be coming through soon with them little turkey quiches. Maybe we can *inspect* a couple of trays."

Roger agreed, and the ravenous pair exited the Office of Kitchen Stuff in search of inspectable quiche.

"Was *that* just an inconvenience?" said Tuck as the office door slammed shut.

Milo thought about it. They were fine, weren't they? Nothing terrible had happened. "Yeah, I think it was."

"And what about getting down from here? Is that just an inconvenience too?"

Milo shrugged. "Guess we'll find out." He patted Gilgamesh's feathers. "Hey, buddy. Great job getting us up here. Think you could get us down now?"

The turkey snorted and shifted its weight beneath them.

"It's sleeping," said Tuck.

"Buddy?" Milo patted a little harder. "Gilgamesh? Chirrup?" Startled, the great bird leaped to attention, sending the lamp swinging once more. *Wurble!* With a lurch, they half sailed, half tumbled from their perch. Tuck and Milo held on until impact, when they bounced off Gilgamesh's back and landed in a heap atop the worktable.

"Oh, no, you're right," said Tuck, rubbing her head. "That was *very* convenient."

Tuck's statement was accurate. It was quite convenient that they had landed atop the worktable, just as it had been convenient that the security ogre had emptied the Kitchen Stuff toolbox upon it. Already, Milo was digging through the pile of wrenches, screwdrivers, measuring tapes, and hammers. "There's got to be a pencil or two in here." He grunted and shoved aside a pair of pliers. "Come help."

Tuck, however, was strolling across the tabletop. "One-man job," she said. "You keep on. I'll secure the perimeter."

It did not feel like a one-man job. Many of the tools were as large as Milo, and most were heavy.

Finally, near the bottom of the pile, he found three pencils. One was long and unsharpened, one was nothing more than a stub, and the third was somewhere between the two. Milo saw the flaw in his plan. Pencils had been the first thing that came to mind, and he had given some thought as to how two or three pencils bound together might be thick enough to block the whazzit from opening completely, but he hadn't given any thought to their length. What if they were too long to fit in the space? What if they were so short they popped out of place when the whazzit sprang open? There had been no scale markers on the diagram. He couldn't be sure. And if he was wrong, they'd be risking everything for nothing.

"Incoming!" cried Tuck.

Milo heard a sproinging sound and looked up just in time to see a roll of cellophane tape the size of a trashcan lid zinging toward his head. He crouched as it whizzed past.

"Woo-hoo!" cheered Tuck. "Did you see that?"

Milo lifted his head. "What are you doing?"

Tuck was standing on the far side of the worktable next to a battered toaster that had been knocked onto its side. "As long as those security ogres are off getting snacks, we should have a little fun. It's a toaster catapult! Isn't it cool? Watch!"

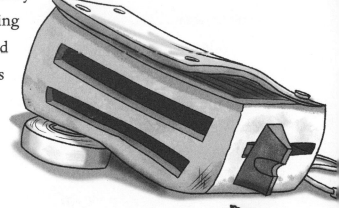

Tuck loaded another roll of tape into the bread slot. With both hands, she pulled back the lever on the toaster's side and . . . "Bombs away!" The tape roll shot into the air.

Wurble-wurble! Gilgamesh flapped his wings and glided to the relative safety of the Kitchen Stuff floor.

Tuck readied a battered calculator for flight. "Who's the mechanical genius now, Pencil Boy?"

"I never said I was a mechanical genius. In fact—" *Spro-ing!* The calculator soared overhead. "Um, in fact, I'm not sure my plan is going to work."

"Because we'll get caught? Or because the idea of jamming something with pencils is stupid?"

"The second one," said Milo. "The pencils." He watched as Tuck tossed a paper plate over her shoulder and searched for something else to launch. "It's just that there's no room for error. We can't make the pencils bigger or smaller once we get there. We're stuck with what we bring. And if it doesn't fit, then . . ."

"Rigidity is the mark of a faulty plan," said Tuck, sliding something silvery—a blender lid, perhaps—into the toaster. "Lyndon says that's in the manual: A good mission is a flexible mission, one that lets you adjust to circumstances." She let the silver disk fly. It pinged against a shelf of can openers.

"A record for the champ!" Tuck raised both arms and waved at an imaginary crowd of fans.

How could Milo be flexible? Even if he had located a whole raft of pencils, there were only so many that he and Tuck could carry, and there was no knowing which would be the right length.

"I really pulled back on that one," Tuck called. "Let me do a couple more before you say the oath, okay?"

"Yeah. Okay." Milo did not want to call the zipper, but what choice did he have? His idea was not going to work. Pencils. What had he been thinking?

He *hadn't* been thinking. He had been so desperate to convince Tuck that he had said the first thing that popped into his head.

Zing-zing! Two rolls of tape shot from the toaster, though neither sailed as high or as far as the first roll had. "Takes more muscle to shoot two," said Tuck.

"There's more weight for the springs to . . ." said Milo. "The *springs!* Tuck, that's it!"

"I'd say 'What's it?,' but I'm afraid you'll sing again."

"The springs! They're flexible! They can expand or contract to fit the space, and they'll bend in any direction we need." He pictured the dryer diagram again, imagining the space the springs would need to fill in order to keep the whazzit from opening. Springs would work. He was sure of it. Pretty sure, anyway.

"I was all ready to go home," said Tuck. "Now you want me to go looking for springs?"

Milo grabbed one of the smaller screwdrivers and dragged it over to the beat-up toaster. Its plastic exterior had cracked, and it was easy enough for Milo to peer inside. "There are at least six springs in there. They're squished up right now, but they look plenty long. All we have to do is pry this open."

"Seems like a one—"

"It's a two-man job," Milo said, wedging the flat head of the screwdriver deep into the crack. "Come over here and sit down. Please."

Tuck did as Milo asked. They sat side by side on the worktable, their feet pressed against the toaster, pulling back on the screwdriver's handle again and again as if it were an enormous oar. At last, a satisfying *crack* rang out and the toaster's plastic cover popped out of place.

"Now we can get to work," said Milo.

"Now?" Tuck wiped her forehead. "What were we doing before?"

Together, they unscrewed screws and lifted out parts

until they were able to pull six sproingy coils from the belly of the machine.

Once freed of their toaster confines, the springs proved to be quite long—much longer than any of the pencils had been. "Have you thought about how we're supposed to carry those?" asked Tuck.

Milo had. First, he nested three coils together so that they interlocked. "Help me smoosh them down."

Smooshing turned out to be difficult. The springs were strong, and it took both him and Tuck to compress them. Milo found a box of thick rubber bands and stretched several of them over and around the springs until they were bound so tight that they were no bigger than a school backpack. He did the same with the second trio of springs.

"This ought to do it," said Milo. He lifted a coil and slipped his arm and head through one of the rubber bands. The springs hung like a quiver of arrows on his back.

"Put yours on, Tuck, and we can get out of here." Milo walked to the edge of the table. "Hey, Gilgamesh!" he called to the bird below. "C'mon up!" The turkey paid him no heed, wandering instead toward the pile of toasters, pecking about in search of crumbs.

"Come!" said Milo again.

The bird ignored him.

"We're going to have to rappel," said Tuck.

"What?"

"Rappel. You know. Like rock climbers going down a cliff?"

"You know how to do that?"

"I've done it. Once. We'll need some rope."

Milo searched the tool pile and located a cloth measuring tape. "Will this work?" he asked.

Tuck nodded. "It'll have to." She knotted one end of the tape around the handle of a heavy-looking blender.

"How long ago did you last do this?" asked Milo.

"A few years. My ninth birthday. You can be a junior agent when you're nine. There are lots of things kids can do that adults can't, like spotting brownies and fairy resuscitation." Tuck pulled hard on the tape, testing the strength of her knot. "My father had forgotten it was my birthday. When he found out, he asked what I wanted as a present, and I said I wanted to go on a mission with him. I don't think he'd have said yes, but he was feeling guilty. He and a small team were headed to an abandoned troll mountain and it wasn't considered risky, so I got to go. Let's see if this is long enough."

Tuck hurled the tape over the table edge and listened as it

slapped on the floor below. "Perfect. Help me pull this back up." Milo grabbed hold of the tape and hauled it up, length by length, as Tuck continued her story.

"When my father was a kid, he was naturally gifted and didn't need much training. I guess he expected me to be the same and to keep up with all the hiking and tracking and climbing. I did my best—I was good at climbing—but I got tired. We were walking along this forest trail, and I was falling farther and farther behind and it was getting dark, and next thing I know, I'm standing at the edge of a cliff all alone." Tuck held the end of the measuring tape out to Milo. "You want to go first?"

Milo shook his head. "Maybe I should watch you?"

She threaded the cloth tape between her back and the toaster springs and wrapped it around her middle, knotting it twice. "My dad and the other agents had started over the cliff, and the last agent in the party was already about twenty feet down. It was Lyndon. When he looked up and saw me, he just hung there for a minute—probably debating what would happen to him if he disobeyed my father's original order to head down the mountain—but he came back up and got me."

"And he taught you how to rappel," said Milo.

Tuck paused. "No. I guess he didn't, really. He just put me over his shoulder and said, 'Trust me,' and I did."

"Wait a minute — so you haven't really done this before?"

Tuck tested the rope knot again. "You just have to hold on to the rope — or the tape, in this case — and sort of walk backwards down the cliff — or the table leg — letting out the rope as you go."

"I don't know about this . . ." said Milo.

"You want to call the zipper?"

Milo did not.

"Okay, then." Tuck took a second to polish her Excellence medal, then lowered herself over the edge of the table. Milo watched as slowly, step after step, she descended, until finally her feet touched ground. "I did it!" Tuck performed a celebratory chicken dance as she undid the knot at her waist. *"I did it! I did it!"* she sang. "Your turn, Junior Speck."

Milo pulled the tape up and slipped it under the springs as Tuck had done, knotting it tightly around his chest. The floor looked twice as far away as it had a moment ago, but if Tuck could rappel, surely he could. He knotted the tape again. *Quank,* warned the ducky.

Milo lay down on his belly and backed over the side of the tabletop, like a swimmer easing into a too-chilly pool.

He wrapped the tape twice around his forearm, then grabbed hold as tightly as he could before letting the slack drop down beneath him.

"Now put your feet on the table leg," coached Tuck, "and lean back. Easy! That's good. Just walk backwards—and don't let go of the rope!"

Perhaps it was his slippers, or maybe the exhaustion from the day, but Milo's descent from the table was nowhere near as simple as Tuck's had been. Again and again, he lost his footing, and again and again he swung out of control, crashing against the table leg. Milo reached the end of his rope before he reached the end of the tape. His slipper slipped, his grip failed, and he fell the last few ogre inches, landing with a thud.

"That was kind of embarrassing," said Tuck. "You okay?"

Milo got to his feet. He was bruised and his legs shook

with fatigue, but nothing was broken, as far as he could tell. "Yeah. I guess."

"Good." Tuck returned her gaze to a broken waffle iron in which she had been examining her reflection. "I wish Lyndon could have seen me."

"I bet he'd get the board to reinstate you immediately," said Milo.

"Huh? Oh, yeah, the board. I bet they'd be impressed too." Tuck put her fists on her hips and lifted her chin in action-figure pose. She gave herself a steely glare, then turned back to Milo. "What's next?"

Milo was not sure. They had the springs they needed to foil the whazzit, and he was almost certain that the gap in the back of the SuperDry 2000 was wide enough for them to slip inside. But how were they to get to the SuperDry 2000 without being seen? And what if they were too late and the whazzit had already been installed when they arrived?

Milo knew the answer. He'd call the zipper and they'd go home.

He caught his reflection in the waffle iron. A bruise purpled on his forehead. His ducky shirt was still flecked with turkey bits, and his corduroys and slippers, once soggy with mayonnaise, were now caked in thick, linty dust. He looked nothing like a Tuckerman Agent, and after his less-than-spectacular descent from the worktable, he felt no closer to convincing Tuck he should be one.

He still needed to destroy the whazzit. And when he did, everything would be different.

One step at a time, he told himself.

"First, we get out of here," said Milo.

20

Someone's Coming!

Perched atop Gilgamesh, Milo and Tuck exited the Office of Kitchen Stuff slowly, the door bumping against them with every tiny step and finally closing with a soft *click*.

"Okay, pal, let's go." Milo tugged the shoelace rein to the right.

He tried not to worry about his lack of a plan for getting to the SuperDry 2000. *Flexibility is the hallmark of a good agent,* he reminded himself. Too bad he wasn't a real agent at all.

Tuck did not seem a bit nervous. Milo could hear her singing the chicken dance tune quietly to herself. *"Wait till Lyndon hears about this. Wait till Lyndon hears about this. He'll be so proud. Da da da da."*

A *ka-chunk* echoed behind them.

"Someone's coming!" whispered Tuck.

Milo scanned the hallway. The broken elevator was still

a long way away, and all the office doors remained closed. There were no trashcans or chairs to hide behind—but just ahead was the OUT OF ODOR drinking fountain he had seen earlier. It was the boxy metal kind and was suspended an ogre foot off the ground, leaving a space beneath just large enough, Milo hoped, for a determined turkey to squish into. He yanked on the reins, urging Gilgamesh toward it. "Duck," he said.

Gilgamesh warbled, but did not move.

"I'm not calling you a duck. I'm saying . . . oh, forget it. Tuck, we've got to get off him."

In an instant they had tumbled off the great bird's back and, using the shoelace as a lead, pulled and prodded until Gilgamesh was sufficiently squished into the shadowy space beneath the fountain.

"Sit. Plotz, that is," said Milo. "Stay."

Gilgamesh sat and stayed, even as Milo and Tuck wedged themselves between him and the wall.

"Well," said Tuck. "This is cozy." Her voice was muffled, for she—like Milo—was completely engulfed in feathers.

Milo brushed aside a tail feather and peered down the long hallway. The exit door had been propped open, and a pair of ogres in white shirts and black pants were spreading cloth over a two-tiered cart. A third ogre handed them an enormous domed platter, which they set upon the cloth.

"Them Big Wigs are waiting," she said. "You two take the quiches. I'll bring the drumsticks in a few minutes."

The first two catering ogres followed orders, but not without difficulty, as each of the cart's four wheels traveled at its own pace and direction, making it a challenge to steer. The cart shuddered and swerved. Milo worried a little less about being spotted, for the catering ogres' full attention was on the twin tasks of keeping their quiches from crashing to the ground and barking insults at each other.

If the food was being delivered, surely the show was about to start. "Tuck," Milo whispered, "what time is it?"

The feathers glowed, and although Milo could not see her, he knew that Tuck had turned on her ZoomBaby. "Just a second. I—oh!" Tuck gasped.

"What?" asked Milo. "It's late, isn't it? We've got to hurry."

"No, look! He's here!" Tuck pushed her ZoomBaby through Gilgamesh's feathers toward Milo. On the screen was the gray grid of the Tracker, Tuck's fat red dot at the center. But now the two other dots Tuck had noted earlier were larger and had almost reached the middle of the screen.

"It's Lyndon!" said Tuck. "I know it! It's Lyndon! He

recovered your dad's ZoomBaby under the bucket and is on his way here for me. He couldn't find me before, because I had this thing turned off to save the battery, but now—"

The ZoomBaby disappeared through the feathers.

"Wait!" called Milo, but Tuck had already abandoned the safety of the drinking fountain and was running in the direction the dot had indicated. "Lyndon!" Milo heard her call. "Lyndon! I'm here!"

Gilgamesh, startled by the outburst, warbled nervously and smooshed himself farther under the fountain. Milo was knocked to the ground and then sat upon.

"Tuck!" Milo called from beneath the bird. "Come back! You don't know—" Before he could finish his thought, an office door banged open.

"Which way?" growled an unmistakably ogre-ish voice.

The reply was not ogre-ish at all. It did not growl, nor did it boom. It was a quieter voice, though there was something commanding about it. "Right in front of you," it said.

Milo peeked out from under Gilgamesh as best he could. There in the hallway, towering above Tuck, stood two massive security ogres, one of whom carried a silver breakfast tray. Milo watched in horror as the other crouched, his paw-like hands poised to scoop up Tuck.

"Stop!"

The voice may have been smaller and less growly than an ogre's, but it had its effect. The ogre froze midscoop.

"Set me down."

The breakfast tray was lowered to the floor. What rested upon it was not breakfast at all, but a human-sized desk and a human-sized chair, upon which sat a human-sized human dressed in a Tuckerman Agency uniform.

"Lyndon!" cried Tuck.

"My girl!" The man at the desk stood. He had thick, wavy hair and an equally dense mustache, below which sat a smile so broad that it seemed not to belong to him. It was as if he had borrowed a larger man's teeth for the day.

Milo watched as Tuck ran up onto the tray and straight into Lyndon's arms. "I knew you'd come!" said

Tuck. "I knew you had a plan. These two ogres are on your side, aren't they? You got them on your side and you came to get me."

"Exactly right," said Lyndon. "You are a very smart girl. Very clever, too. You escaped from your prison." He lifted a ZoomBaby off his desk. "Clever idea to leave this on Voice Activate."

Even through turkey feathers, Milo could see how proud Tuck looked.

"Very impressive," Lyndon continued. "And letting those other kids free? That was you? You did this all by yourself?"

Milo waited for Tuck to introduce him and explain how they had been working together to destroy the whazzit, but Tuck only shrugged.

She's not going to tell him about me, thought Milo. *She's going to let him think she escaped from the bucket and rescued Jane and Ernesto and Little Dude from their cage all by herself.* He bet she was even going to go off with this Lyndon guy and his ogre pals now, leaving Milo to call the zipper and go home alone.

He fought the urge to wriggle out from under Gilgamesh and call Tuck a fraud. He didn't need credit, he reminded himself. All he needed was to stay an agent so he could help Dad find Mom. Maybe it was better this way. If Tuck lied to

Lyndon about what she had accomplished, there was no way she would fire Milo. Not when he knew the truth about how things had really happened and could spill the beans at any time.

"And you've been acquiring things too, eh?" said Lyndon, tugging gently at the rubber band that stretched over Tuck's shoulder.

"Well . . ." started Tuck.

"Boss? I think they're calling for you." The security ogre had a finger in one ear and wore a small receiver in the other.

"You *think* they're calling?" said Lyndon.

"That or somebody's ordering at the McGobbler's across the street—these headsets don't work too good."

"We will assume it is the former." Lyndon smoothed his mustache and turned to Tuck. "There is a very important announcement about to be made—" he began.

"I know!" said Tuck. "About the dryer and everything. About kids being brought here for food."

Lyndon nodded. "You are far smarter than I even knew. It's really too bad we didn't have more time for training. You might have been useful—"

"I can be useful!" insisted Tuck. "You're going in there to destroy the dryer, right? I can help!"

"Now, now, don't get too excited. Have a seat." Lyndon sat Tuck in his chair. "And let's get this thing off you." The man lifted one of Tuck's arms and, like a father helping his young child remove a too-tight sweater, pulled the rubber band up over her head. Then, with startling speed, he stretched the band down over both of Tuck's arms and around the back of the chair, pinning her in place.

"Hey!" cried Tuck. "What are you doing? I'll stay out of your way! If you don't want my help, just say so."

"I do want your help. You will be very helpful, dear. Your replacement is late being delivered, and it was going to be difficult for those Big Wigs to focus if they thought there would be no Squashing. Now perhaps they'll listen to my presentation, believing that they'll get the show they came for."

Milo fought the alarm rising in his chest. Lyndon must mean to trick the ogres, he told himself. It must be part of a larger plan—Tuck would be offered for the Squashing as if everything was normal. That's why she had to be rubber-banded to the chair, so she looked like a prisoner, right? Lyndon and his ogres would destroy the whazzit, and then he and Tuck and whoever else was in on the plan—maybe even Dad—would all escape together. That *had* to be it.

Lyndon's voice grew commanding again. "Bring this child in and tell them that I have recaptured Tuckerman. I will use the backstage entrance and stay there until I am properly introduced."

The second ogre nodded so firmly that his mirrored glasses bobbled on his nose. "Anything you say, Dr. El."

21

Dr. El

Dr. El?

Milo and Tuck gasped simultaneously, though Milo's gasp went unheard by anyone but the turkey who sat atop him.

"You see, dear," said Lyndon, his borrowed-looking smile growing even larger, "having you Squashed helps me in two ways. First, it satisfies the bloodlust of the good citizens of Ogregon. They do love a good Squashing, and since this is my first real appearance among them, I want everything to go perfectly. You don't really get a second chance with ogres. Mess up, and they eat you. This presentation of the whazzit is my chance to persuade all Ogregon of my power and brilliance . . . and after that's done, their world will be pretty much at my command. Once I've made friends here, it will be easy to align myself with the trolls and the orcs and whoever else I might need."

"Need for what?" asked Tuck.

"Credible threat. In the old days, everyone at Home knew about dragons and goblins and what have you. Those who offered protection were heroes. They were revered. Honored. Stories were told about them, books were written. They were well compensated for their deeds too. But today, your average homeowner goes about la-di-da, working at his job, shopping at the grocery store, never once thinking he might run into a bloodthirsty orc in the frozen food section. Never once realizing the importance of those with the skills and know-how to save them." Lyndon paused to smooth his hair. "I intend to change that."

"You can't—" started Tuck.

"Not yet. But here's the second benefit to your Squashing: Once the deed is done and there is no remaining Tuckerman heir, power will shift, as it has in ages past, to the next most qualified agent, which is, of course, me. Finally, the Agency will have the leader it deserves, and I will have the power that should have been mine all along."

"But . . . I trusted you!"

"Yes, you did, and I really need to thank you for that.

You *and* your father. Him so lazy about anything that wasn't a super-fun adventure and you so needy after his neglect. I couldn't believe my luck when he heard about that frost dragon. All I had to say was 'Don't send two when one will do,' and he was out of the picture. And you? You're just a kid. It won't be hard to persuade our fellow agents that you ordered me to take you here to Ogregon and then escaped to follow your own selfish pursuits."

Lyndon dropped his smile and made his face sorrowful, convincing tears streaming down his cheeks. "She was so young. So impulsive. Terrible tragedy." He pulled a handkerchief from his pocket and wiped his eyes. "The makeup people will have to go waterproof for that press conference. Can't have the new Head of the Tuckerman Agency looking too much of a mess, can we?"

In the stories that Milo and his father had read, there was often a moment like this, one when time seemed to stop as the villain explained his evil plan. Those moments always bothered Milo—why didn't the hero attack? Why did he just sit there listening? And yet that was exactly what was happening now. Milo was just lying there listening, unable to move—not only because of the outsized turkey that sat atop him—but because he was stunned by what he was hearing. Tuck, too, sat frozen, as if waiting for Lyndon's words to reorganize themselves into any other meaning than that she had been betrayed.

"I trusted you," she said again.

"We've covered that," said Lyndon. He snapped his fingers. "Okay, boys, let's get going."

The larger of the security ogres lifted the breakfast tray from the Home Office floor, and the frozen feeling that had so paralyzed Tuck and Milo vanished.

Tuck struggled to free herself from the desk chair.

Milo struggled to get himself out from under Gilgamesh.

Gilgamesh struggled to push himself farther under the drinking fountain.

And the rubber bands—which had been holding Milo's tightly compressed toaster springs—struggled free of their duty.

Zoing! The springs exploded to full length, snapping the already-skittish bird sharply in the backside. Gilgamesh shot from under the fountain like a plumed cannonball, flapping and wurbling and scattering dust in all directions. The startled ogres screamed and threw up their hands. The breakfast tray launched high into the air, turning end over end, sending both Lyndon and the chair-bound Tuck flying.

With reflexes a thousand times quicker than his wit, a security ogre snatched his boss in midair—but Tuck continued skyward, turning pinwheel-esque. Milo stood paralyzed. What could he do? He couldn't catch her. He couldn't stop her from falling. He was helpless.

"Come!" A strong, firm voice befitting the Head of the Tuckerman Agency cut through the chaos. Gilgamesh rocketed straight for the free-falling girl. Milo watched in awe as the great bird opened its beak, caught the arm of the chair mid-tumble, and soared down the hallway, through the propped-open exit door, and out of sight.

The breakfast tray clattered to the floor, the desk and the security ogre's headset crashing down beside it. *"Dr. El to the*

Green Room for makeup," screeched a voice from the headset. Milo crouched reflexively under the fountain as a security ogre scooped up the device.

"What?" he hollered into it. "Okay. Dr. El, the replacement boy got delivered. And they need you in makeup."

"Well then, to makeup we shall go," said Lyndon.

"Don't you want we should go after Tuckerman?"

"One of you take me to the Green Room, and the other can go after her, I suppose—but if you don't find her right away, just come back. Now that the replacement has been delivered, we won't need to Squash her. The bird is probably halfway to the forest by now, and the girl is as good as dead. She's completely clueless about how to survive on her own." Milo heard Lyndon chuckle. "I should know. I trained her."

22

Tuckerman Agents Are on the Way!

Milo stood stunned as the security ogres parted, one heading toward the Office of Bragging About Stuff with Lyndon —Dr. El—and the other lumbering down the long Home Office home office hallway and out the exit door, slamming it hard behind him.

Milo slumped against the cold, damp wall. Tuck was out there all alone and there was nothing Milo could do. He couldn't open that huge door all by himself. And even if he could, then what? How would he begin to know where to look for her?

He could have stopped this from happening. If he'd done what his father told him to do, if he'd gone through the zipper with Jane or called the zipper himself once he had been sworn in as an emergency agent, Tuck would be safe.

But no, he had wanted to go on adventures. He had wanted to be such a big hero that Tuck would make him a real agent.

Who did he think he was? He was a kid. A scrawny little kid.

He was not some hero in a book.

How stupid he had been.

There was nothing he could do about it either, except call the zipper and go back to Tuckerman Agency Headquarters and cross his fingers that some real agent would show up so he could explain everything. Hopefully, it would not be too late for a true hero to zip to Ogregon and save Tuck. Wherever she was.

Though there were no ogres around to hear him, Milo could not bring himself to speak in anything more than a whisper. "I swear as a Tuckerman Agent to do my duty with courage and wisdom and utmost fidelity, until all that can be done has been done."

The silver light appeared. It grew wider and sharper until the gleaming zipper hung before him, its shining ring dangling within reach. All the while, the words of the oath echoed beneath the fountain. *Until all that can be done has been done.*

Milo grabbed hold of the ring and dragged it slowly to the floor.

Just as before, he saw the golden fizzy light and the wood-paneled room with the painting of the needle-holding knight. Unlike before, a stern recorded voice echoed off its walls: "HALT! TUCKERMAN AGENTS ARE ON THE WAY! THERE IS NO ESCAPE!" In the midst of it all, on the desk closest to the zipper opening, a plump, dark-haired boy sat swinging his legs and munching happily on a granola bar.

"Little Dude?" said Milo.

The boy looked up from his snack. His eyes grew round, and bits of oat and chocolate chip flew through the air as he cried out. "*¡Patito!*"

From somewhere out of Milo's view came Ernesto's voice. "Little Dude, I don't know where Patito is, but I found some potato chips." The boy walked up to the desk carrying an armload of snacks. "Oh! Hey!" he said, spotting the zipper. "Jane, look! They're okay!"

Milo watched as Jane hurried over. "Milo! What happened? We were worried! I tried to come back for you guys, but I couldn't get that zipper thing to work."

"Your mission failed. You said 'to get us *all* out of Ogregon,' and then I messed that up for you."

"No problem, man. Now that I know you're okay, I don't have any reason to go back there. Ever."

"HALT! TUCKERMAN AGENTS ARE ON THE WAY!" boomed the recording.

Little Dude put his hands over his ears. "Halt," he said.

"Hey," said Jane. "Where's Tuck?"

"She's . . . I don't know." Milo explained as quickly as he could about staying behind to sabotage the whazzit. About Lyndon being Dr. El, and Tuck escaping with Gilgamesh. "I don't know where she is now," he said finally. "I called the zipper so I could go to the Agency and find help—"

"THERE IS NO ESCAPE!" interrupted the alarm.

"How long has that been going on?" Milo asked.

"A few minutes. We've been locked in this room ever since we got here, and Little Dude was hungry. We started searching the desks for snacks, and we must have triggered some kind of alarm."

"I found granola bars," said Ernesto. "Want one?" The boy tossed a foil package at the zipper opening, but instead of reaching Milo, it bounced back.

"I guess nothing can get through until someone says a mission," said Milo.

"So, state your mission and come home," said Jane.

Milo hesitated.

"It's easy," said Jane. "Just say whatever it is you want to do."

What *did* he want to do? Milo could think of lots of things he wanted. He wanted Tuck to be safe and his whole family to be home in Downriver, together again. But what did he want to *do?*

"TUCKERMAN AGENTS ARE ON THE WAY!"

The silver ring jiggled.

"Hurry up, man. It's gonna close."

Milo took a step toward the zipper opening. His legs felt slow and heavy, and once again he was reminded of climbing the snow-covered hill behind Guinevere's Pizza and Subs. "I can't come back yet. My dad is still here. I want to be here with him. You'll tell the agents what I told you, though, won't you? You'll tell them to come find Tuck?"

All this time the zipper pull had been slowly rising. Jane hopped up on a desk to keep Milo in view. "I'll tell them."

"And tell them they can't trust Lyndon—he wants to take over the Agency—they've got to stop him. And about the whazzit, too, okay? Tell them to go to the Bragging Office. Tell them to destroy the whazzit. Tell them—" He was on his toes now, peering up through the ever-shrinking opening. He saw the top of Jane's head nod.

"I'll tell them everything," Jane called back. "But what are you going to do?"

The zipper reached the end of its track. Milo watched it shimmer and then dissolve.

What *was* he going to do?

Milo wasn't sure. All he knew was that he could not leave Ogregon until he was certain that Dad was safe.

As if on cue, the doors at the far end of the hallway banged open.

Milo whipped around. A catering ogre emerged in the open doorway, pushing a cart upon which rested a tower of turkey drumsticks so tall that she was forced to peer around it to see where she was going. Milo watched as the cart approached, its sticky wheels sending it zigging and zagging down the Home Office home office hallway just as the quiche cart had earlier.

200

Now's my chance, thought Milo, and for once he knew for what. The cart was headed toward him, bound for the Office of Bragging About Stuff. If he could sneak under the tablecloth onto the cart's bottom shelf, he'd be wheeled right inside that room.

When the cart got close enough to the fountain, he decided, he would dash out of hiding and make a dive for it. With any luck, the catering ogre would be so focused on trying to steer that she would not notice a very small boy. And if she did . . . well, Milo would think about that if the time came.

The cart drew nearer. Milo prepared himself as it swerved wide, then angled toward him. The catering ogre cursed, and the drumstick platter rattled louder.

One . . . thought Milo. *Two* . . . *Three!*

He leaped from under the fountain, sprinted alongside the cart, and dove for the flapping tablecloth. *Wham!* His chest hit the bottom tier of the cart, nearly knocking the wind from him, but he managed to grab hold of the cloth. He swung one foot and then the other up onto the shelf. The cart swerved again, and Milo was flung forward so violently that he lost his grip and landed spread-eagle beside a tray of rattling cutlery, the tablecloth fluttering back into place behind him.

Milo dropped his head and closed his eyes. He had done it. He was sweaty and battered and could hardly breathe, but he had done it.

"Nice work, Junior Speck."

Milo looked up. There was Tuck, sitting cross-legged on a stack of napkins. Bent over her, looking more than uncomfortable in the not-quite-turkey-sized space, was Gilgamesh.

"You're safe! I can't believe it! Are you okay?"

"What?" Tuck cupped her ear. The rumbling of the cart and the rattling of the cutlery made it difficult to hear.

Milo crawled over to sit beside her on the napkin stack. "I said, are you okay?"

"My pants are covered in muck, and Big Bird needs a bath, but we're fine." Tuck reached up to pat the neck of the turkey. "Aren't we, fella?"

Wurble-wurble, said Gilgamesh.

They did look worse for their time outdoors. Tuck's jacket was gone except for its lapel, which dangled pathetically from the Excellence medal that kept the scrap pinned to her shirt. Her hands and face were smudged with dirt. Gilgamesh's feathers were covered with sticks and dried leaves.

"What happened?"

"You saw how this guy swooped me away, right?"

Milo nodded.

"Well, soon as we glide outside, he drops me in a bush." Tuck patted the turkey's neck again. "And I'm all, *That's it. I'm a goner. Some ogre will find me and eat me, or I'll just hang here in a boxwood hedge, rubber-banded to a desk chair until I starve to death.* And you know, Junior Speck, I was almost okay with it. I mean, it wasn't like I wanted to die, but . . . you know. My dad is gone. I'm an embarrassment of an agent. I was completely duped by a person I trusted . . ." Tuck sniffed. "Forget that . . . it's classified."

"By Lyndon," said Milo. "You don't have to pretend it's classified. I saw everything."

Tuck ignored him. "Next thing I know, Gilgamesh is pulling at those rubber bands on my back like they're the juiciest worms he's ever seen. *Snip-snap.* I'm free-falling through branches. My jacket gets snagged—rips, comes right off—I'm getting scratches everyplace."

Tuck held up her arm so he could see the crosshatches of angry red lines. "And then I land—*whomp*—in this big pile of mulch. Mulch makes a pretty cushy landing surface—remember that if you ever need to drop from a height five times your own."

Milo said he would, but silently hoped he'd never have to.

"So I'm lying there, looking through branches up at the sky, trying to catch my breath, when the building door slams. I flip over onto my stomach to take a look, but then this bird sits on me like I need hatching. I can't see anything, but I can hear that security ogre calling me. 'TUUUCKERMAN! TUUUUUUCKERMAN!' Out of nowhere this other ogre hollers for him to shut up, he's giving her a migraine. Her," said Tuck, pointing to where, just beyond the tablecloth, the catering ogre pushed the wobbly cart. "She was the hollerer. And he says, 'You shut up,' and she says, 'No, you shut up,' and he says, 'Hey, are those drumsticks?' And she says, 'Yeah, want one?' And then it gets quiet except for these terrible chewing sounds. I crawl out from under Gilgamesh and get to the end of the hedge, where I can see them both. They're eating drumstick after drumstick, crunching and gnawing and drooling and tossing the bones over their shoulders. It's awful to look at. Awful to hear. And I start thinking about how that would have happened to Jane if you hadn't set her free. And to Ernesto and Little Dude. I finally start thinking about all those other kids, real kids with real lives elsewhere, who are gonna get sucked through that dryer and eaten. All because of *him*."

"Lyndon," said Milo.

Tuck nodded. "Anyway, my springs got caught up in the hedge somewhere, and I figured that after everything you'd seen you'd zipped off anyway, but I thought if I could find your dad, I could get him to zip me to Headquarters and we could get some agents—real, trained, dedicated agents who know what they're doing—and send them back here."

Beyond the tablecloth, the catering ogre swore and the cart swerved again, throwing them all off balance. A pair of hors d'oeuvre forks bounced from their tray and clattered to a spot beside Milo.

"So, while those two dopes were focused on eating, Gilgamesh and I snuck in here," said Tuck, patting her napkin seat. "I'm surprised you didn't go home."

"I almost did." Milo explained about calling the zipper and seeing Jane and the boys.

"So, she's sending agents?" said Tuck. "And you stayed here because of your dad."

The wheels of the catering cart groaned as it turned a corner. Milo heard ogre voices—lots of them.

". . . last explosion singed her eyebrows right off. Draws them on with a paintbrush now."

205

". . . not the heat, it's the humidity. It's murder on my curls . . ."

". . . That gang of pixies in '09? Now, *that* was a Squashing. Green on the inside, pixies. Who knew?"

The hum of voices grew louder. The cart was just outside the Office of Bragging About Stuff, Milo was sure of it.

"Big announcement?" said another voice. "Big deal. Squash Tuckerman and call it a day, I say."

Tuck shuddered and closed her eyes.

It would be bad enough, Milo knew, to hear ogres talking about how much they wanted to see you Squashed, but to know that Squashing had been planned by the person you trusted most in the world? He could not imagine it. There had been times, of course, that he had been angry at Mom for leaving, but he had never really felt betrayed by her. And even if he had, Milo knew Dad was always with him — even when his father was away. What would it be like to live without that feeling?

"Hey, Tuck," said Milo. "You know what? We can go back now, if you want. Our springs are gone and there's nothing we can do about the whazzit. I can zip us home now, and you can talk to your agents and we can just get out of here."

Tuck pushed a wave of hair behind her ear. "I thought you wanted to be near your dad."

"I do," Milo admitted. "But it's not right of me to keep you here."

The Head of the Tuckerman Agency looked at him for a long time. Then she unfastened her Excellence badge and pinned it to his ducky sweatshirt.

"What's this for?" asked Milo.

"Excellence, Junior Speck. Duh. Don't give me a reason to take it back." She tossed the remains of her lapel over her shoulder. "We'll stay, at least until the other agents get here. Maybe we'll learn something that will help them catch Lyndon. But you have to promise me—"

"First sign of trouble."

23

Plans and Explanations

As the catering ogre shoved her drumstick-laden cart into the Bragging Office, Milo and Tuck crept to the edge of the shelf and lifted the cloth just high enough to peek out from under it.

It was difficult to see more than ogre shoes, but there were a great number of those clomping about. An instrumental version of the whazzit song played as background music, and Milo could hear the slosh and chug of washing machines. The room was warm and humid and smelled like an old rug. Milo wiped a bead of sweat from his brow as the cart came to a stop in the same spot that the janitor's trolley had earlier that day.

As long as things had not been moved since he and Tuck were last here, the coils of television cables would be behind them, Milo knew. He crawled over the displaced hors d'oeuvre forks to the far side of the cart to check. The cables were still there, tucked in the back corner of the room, just a few feet away. The Bragging Office lights had not yet been turned off for the show, but the cart would offer good cover. If he and Tuck were fast, they would not likely be spotted running to them.

"Ready?" he asked.

The Head of the Tuckerman Agency nodded, then dropped over the side of the cart and dashed for safety. Milo grabbed a fork. It was nearly as big as he was, and he had no idea how he'd use it, but somehow holding a weapon in this room full of ogres made him feel just a little bit better. He followed Tuck, sprinting for the cable coils and diving into the pile after her.

"Oof!"

"Sorry, Tuck."

"Don't apologize to *me*."

Milo looked down. "Dad!" he said, dropping his fork in surprise.

Samson Speck crawled out from under his son. "What are you two doing here? Did the oath not work? Where are the other kids?"

"They're at Headquarters. They set off an alarm, and as soon as agents arrive to investigate, Jane's going to send them here to help."

Wurble-wurble. The mulch-covered head of Gilgamesh peered over the cables.

"Hello, old boy. What happened to you?"

"Dad," said Milo. "Somebody's going to see him."

Milo's father whistled softly. A second *wurble* echoed just a few feet away. Gilgamesh tilted his head toward the sound, then followed it.

"Lochinvar is hiding behind the equipment boxes," said

Dad. "There's room for both of them there. Now, tell me what happened."

"We had a little turkey trouble," said Tuck.

Milo explained about Jane and the boys going to Headquarters and Tuck swearing in Milo as an agent and about their idea to block the whazzit with the toaster springs. He felt his cheeks flush with embarrassment as he described his plans. "It turned out to be kind of a waste of time," he said, avoiding his father's eyes.

"Your spring plan?" Dad tapped his foot. "I can't really see it that way, son. Although I wish you'd gone home right away, it seems to me that your planning clarified the threat and offered a possible way to thwart it, and those are both very useful things to share with the rest of the Agency."

"Really?" asked Milo. "You don't think this is just one huge failure? I mean, we didn't even get close to that dryer."

"Sometimes, doing what can be done also means recognizing what can't—at least, not on your own. So, where are these springs now?"

"Mine are under a drinking fountain," said Milo.

"We lost them after we found out about Lyndon," said Tuck.

"What about Lyndon?"

Tuck looked at Milo. "You tell him," she said. "I'm going to, um, secure the perimeter."

Milo watched Tuck climb to the top of the cable coil and peek out over it. "About Lyndon tricking Tuck," he said, quietly. "About him being Dr. El and all that. That's why you're here, right? To stop him?"

"To stop him? To stop *him*," said Dad. "*Him*. Oh, Milo! Dr. El is Lyndon? I knew it had to be a human—no ogre could have . . . but El isn't *E-l*, it's *L!* Dr. El is Lyndon! That rotten sycophantic scumbag. Ha! *Lyndon* betrayed the Agency, not . . ." Milo's father laughed, although the look on his face was not exactly joy. He seemed relieved, and also, maybe, a little sad.

El like the letter L, thought Milo. *Not El, short for* . . . Milo spoke before he even knew what he was saying. "*Eleanor.*"

Dad's eyes met his. "Milo," he said. "I never really—"

"You thought El was short for Eleanor? That's why you're in Ogregon—because you thought Dr. El was Mom!" said Milo. "How could you think—"

"Milo. Listen, son. I had no idea what was really going on here. All the files said was that there was a Dr. El tinkering with the technology. There was some talk of network trouble. For all I knew, your mom was on a top-secret mission. If I'd known about the whazzit, about the kids, I wouldn't have suspected her for a second. Not even brainwashed would she help with such a thing."

"You should have told me. You should have told me about being an agent and about trying to find Mom. You should have told me she was an agent too."

"Shhh, son—"

But Milo would not be shushed. "Do you know what it's like not to know? To wonder if she left because of you? To think maybe you could have done something to get her to stay? Do you?"

"Yes," said Dad. "I do."

"Specks!" Tuck called. "Specks! Come up here and look."

The catering ogre had moved her drumstick cart, leaving a clear view of the room. Several dozen ogres filled the space now, most of them dressed up as if for a party. Their shoes were shiny, their clothes sparkly, and all of them   male and female alike—sported hairdos so massive and elaborate that Milo could only marvel at their architectural genius. Bows and braids supported waterfalls of curls. One was layered like a wedding cake, and another looked exactly like the plastic Christmas tree Grandmother had set up in the living room last December. It even had a star at the top.

"Big Wigs," explained Milo's father.

"No kidding," said Milo.

"Focus, idiot!" hollered a voice. A black beret sailed through the air, and several of the Big Wigs ducked. Despite the ducking, their wigs were still so tall they obscured Milo's view of the lectern, but he could see the silver screen that hung above it, as well as the blurry image that was now projected upon it. The picture on the screen sharpened—and a boy's face, pale and frightened, appeared.

A chant rose up among the Big Wigs. "Squash him! Squash him!"

Milo scanned the room. The television camera was pointing toward the cage that had once held Jane, Ernesto, and Little Dude. "There's another kid in there, Dad!"

"I know, son. They brought him in a few minutes ago. The Home Office is telling everyone he's Tuckerman."

The boy in the cage must be the replacement that Lyndon had mentioned, Milo realized. It could just have easily been Tuck — or Milo. "They're going to Squash him, Dad."

"I intend to get to him before that happens. You and Tuck hid right here earlier, yes? And then made your way to the cages?"

"We ran under the chairs. But, Dad, it was dark then."

"And there weren't so many ogres around," said Tuck.

"They will turn out the lights when the show is about to start. And then I'll do as you did — under the chairs, up the cages, open the latch. Once it's open, I'll slip inside, call the zipper, and take the boy to Headquarters. Look at the Big Wigs. Even now, they're not looking at anything but their quiches and drumsticks. Once the lights go out and the show starts, everyone will be watching the big dryer announcement and no one will notice one tiny man in the dark." Milo's father nodded as if reassuring himself, then smiled at his son. "Does make a fellow wish quality optometry had not been a part of Amos Tuckerman's Big Deal, though."

"My great-grandfather?" asked Tuck.

"Big Deal?" asked Milo.

"I'll explain another time." Dad checked his watch. "It's almost time for the demonstration to start. You and Tuck should go home."

"I want to hear about my great-grandfather," said Tuck.

"You just said it was perfectly safe, Dad. Or were you making that up?"

"I wasn't making anything—It is safe for me—I only—"

Dad looked from Milo to Tuck and back to Milo again. Then he took one more slow look around the ogre-filled room. "Fine," he whispered. "But not up here." He waved for Tuck and Milo to follow him down deep into the cable coil and out of sight.

"Okay, then," said Dad. "Amos Tuckerman's Big Deal."

24

Amos Tuckerman's Big Deal

Dad found a cave-like nook within the cable coils, and they all wedged themselves inside it. Finger to his lips, he listened for any change in ogre activity. Only when he was convinced that they would not be seen or heard, Dad spoke.

"The Ogre Treaty of 1937 is known within the Agency as Amos Tuckerman's Big Deal. Let me back up a little, though." His father's voice grew soft, and Milo was reminded of those evenings long ago when his father would read aloud. "The fabric of space is as old as time. It wears unevenly — small holes and thin spots develop, unexpected forces stress and tear. In the old days, when openings between worlds were discovered, we closed them with buttons and, before that, laces. As you can imagine, things were less contained. Buttons popped. Laces came undone. There were more gaps for Away dwellers to slip through. You don't hear so much about ogres or fairies or elves today as you once did, but that's not because our generation is less superstitious. It's technology. Once the zipper was invented, it became much easier to seal things up."

"So why do you need the Agency at all?" asked Milo. "Why don't you just zip things up permanently?"

"Things go wrong sometimes. Zippers get stuck. Little tears turn into big ones." Milo remembered the ripping sound he had heard as he was pulled into his dryer back home. Is that what had happened to him?

"It's not just that we want to protect our home, son. We have a responsibility to the Aways as well. Take here in Ogregon. Once the zippers were in, ogres couldn't go tromping through space, feasting anywhere they wanted. They were stuck here, and soon they overhunted their land. Many starved. Amos Tuckerman—Priscilla's great-grandfather—tried to help."

Milo glanced at Tuck. She was listening as if this was the first she had heard of her great-grandfather's efforts.

"Amos introduced domesticated animals and tried to teach the ogres how to raise them. As you might guess, it didn't go well. The ogres loved steak and pork so much, they swallowed them all in less than a year. Chickens didn't last much longer. Ogres aren't so fond of turkey, though, and at first, they refused to eat them. This gave the turkeys a head start on establishing a population. Now the farms are full of them. Many turkeys escaped into the wild, so the forests are full of them too, and they aren't as easy to hunt as other animals. Turkeys here are a lot smarter than they are at home."

Milo nodded. Gilgamesh was super smart and he learned quickly, too.

"The Agency helped with other modernizations as well. Electricity. Basic manufacturing. And," said Dad, tapping his temple, "optometry."

"Glasses?"

"They needed to be able to see in order to build things."

Milo thought back to all of the ogres he had seen that day. Every single one of them had been wearing glasses.

"Testing 2, 3 . . . 5 . . ."

Dad scrambled back up to the top of the cable coils, and though he waved them away, Tuck and Milo followed. They peeked cautiously over the edge.

The image on the screen at the front of the room had switched from the frightened boy to the beret-wearing director. "Everybody sit down and shut up! We're gonna start!"

The Big Wigs grumbled as they made their way to their seats.

Dad climbed back down into the coil and motioned for Milo and Tuck to follow him. "Call the zipper now, son," he said when they were safely out of sight. "There's nothing for you to do here, and I need to know that you and Tuck are safe."

"I need to know you're safe too." Milo spoke more loudly than he had intended. "I want to be with you."

"You're always with me," said Milo's father.

"You said that before," said Tuck. "What's it supposed to mean?"

"In my heart. Milo knows this. He is always in my heart, and I am always in his."

"Lovely," said Tuck. "Not really all that helpful when you're outnumbered by security ogres, but lovely."

Milo looked at Tuck, who nodded.

"Tuck and I are staying, Dad," said Milo. "We can help. We can . . ." What could they do?

"We'll keep watch," said Tuck. "If you're spotted, we'll send Lochinvar and Gilgamesh running around all over the place, just like you did for us. We'll create a diversion."

Dad pulled Milo aside. "Son, this is not your responsibility—"

"It's not yours, either! But you're doing it anyway. You're doing what can be done." Milo's father's eyes met his. Milo did not blink. "We can do this," he said. "Tuck and I can help."

The washers chugged, and Milo waited. Finally, his father spoke.

"I'm certain I won't be spotted, but if something were to go wrong, I could use a few seconds of diversion to escape. But Milo, you have got to promise that as soon as I reach that boy, you'll call the zipper and go home. You're sure you can, right? You know how?"

"I already tested it," said Milo, trying not to remember how he had almost abandoned Tuck and Dad earlier.

"Okay. We'll all meet at Headquarters, where we can get an entire division of agents on the case. We'll fill them in on this whazzit thing," Dad said, patting Milo on the shoulder. "And on Lyndon, too, Tuck. You'll tell them what he did to you and what he has planned. And then we'll let them take over. Okay?"

Milo nodded.

Dad looked at Tuck. "Okay, boss?"

Tuck stood taller. "It's a fine plan, Agent Speck."

"Lights!" shouted the director. The overhead lights clicked off, and the spotlights clicked on. "First, an announcement. We got some surprises for you, but no matter what happens, you godda stay in your seats. This is gonna be on TV, and we don't want none of you messing things up, just cuz you get excited about the Squashing or anything."

The Big Wigs muttered discontentedly, but Milo saw the silhouettes of their curls bobbing in assent.

The director turned toward the curtain. "Everybody ready?"

"Ready!" called the ogres behind it. Milo's father used the noise to cover a short, sharp whistle. The shadowy figures of Lochinvar and Gilgamesh appeared in the dark beside the cable coil. "If you need them to run, say 'Allez!' They should take off. And then," he said, looking at Milo very seriously, "so should you."

"Door!" hollered the director. The Office of Bragging About Stuff door slammed shut.

"Camera!" Red lights flashed atop the television camera.

"Action!"

25

The Show Begins

Milo watched as his father crept out of the coil of cables and disappeared into the dark.

He knew the path his father would follow—under the long row of chairs, across a small open aisle, then along the far wall to the cages. *How long will it take until he reaches the boy in the uppermost cage?* Milo wondered. It felt like it had taken forever when he had made the journey, but really, the whole thing could not have lasted very long. How soon would his father be safe? Five minutes? Ten?

"Five, two, four, three, one!" The light on the television camera flickered. Up on the screen, a curtain parted and a gray-haired ogre in a black turtleneck and horn-rimmed glasses emerged. The Big Wigs applauded as he strode to the lectern.

"Hello. I'm Gnash Dashman, president of the Home

Office. I know you're all here for the Tuckerman Squashing, which—I godda say—is gonna be a good one. But before we get to it, the Home Office has a special announcement just for you"—he turned to look directly into the camera —"and for you at home. It's about our brand-new, state-of-the-art clothes-drying system . . . the SuperDry 2000!"

A second spotlight shone, and the image on the screen revealed the enormous dryer. Its door was propped open, and Milo noticed that a screwdriver had been jammed in next to the hinge.

"It looks broke already!" yelled a Big Wig.

"It does, don't it?" said Dashman. "There's a reason for that."

"What is it?" hollered someone else.

"I dunno. But I know who does. Ladies and Gentleogres, shut up and let me introduce our secret surprise guest, the genius behind the SuperDry 2000—oh, you're gonna love this. For the first time ever in public . . . I give you . . . the one and only . . . Dr. El!"

Gasps filled the room as the curtain parted again and a shaggy security ogre stepped forward with a silver tray. The television camera zoomed in as the tray was set upon the lectern and the image of Lyndon filled the screen above. Milo heard Tuck use a word his father reserved for stubbed toes and traffic snarls.

"Hey! It's a human!" hollered one of the Big Wigs.

"It's Tuckerman!" shouted another.

"Dibs!" bellowed several others.

Gnash Dashman leaned over Lyndon and shouted into the mike. "This ain't Tuckerman, you dopes! I just said it was Dr. El, and ain't nobody Squashing him."

"Why not?" demanded a Big Wig. "He looks delicious."

"'Cause he figured out a way to get us more boys, and don't nobody else understand how. Believe me, I tried, and

226

if I'd understood, I'd have had him for lunch myself. No offense, Doc."

Milo watched Dr. El—Lyndon—put on his borrowed-looking smile.

Wait! What was Milo doing watching the man on the screen? He needed to watch for the flash of silver light, so he would know that his father had reached the captive boy and gone home. So that he and Tuck could go home too.

Milo stared through the blackness toward the spot where he knew the cages sat. He did not blink, not even as Lyndon began to speak.

"Dear citizens of Ogregon, as you just heard, I, Prometheus Lyndon—Dr. El, to those who can't seem to remember names—come to you with news that will change your lives forever. An invention so ingenious, so brilliant, it could only have been thought up by me. And it is only out of my desire for your eternal loyalty and friendship that I am bringing it to you. I give you . . . the whazzit!"

Milo kept his eyes turned toward the cages, but he was pretty sure that the image of the gleaming silver whazzit was now spinning on the video screen.

"What's that?" came a shout.

"Whazz-*it*," corrected Lyndon, and he began an

explanation so long and complicated that Milo understood very little of it. The Big Wigs understood even less.

"You're hurting my brains up!"

"Squash him anyway!"

"I'll do it!"

"Wait!" said Lyndon in a voice much less commanding than before. "Wait. Listen. In short, the SuperDry 200 had the power to bring human children from their world to this one."

"What children?"

"You mean boys?"

"Mine never brought no childrens. It just blew up!"

"Exactly." Lyndon raised his voice over their yells. "Nearly all of them just blew up. But the whazzit solves that problem. My invention will allow owners of the new SuperDry 2000 to bring fresh, delicious children to their own homes with every load of laundry—and without a single explosion."

"Prove it!" hollered half the crowd.

"Dibs!" yelled the other.

"I shall prove it! I have reengineered this prototype dryer in such a way as to keep the door open while the dryer runs"—Milo imagined Lyndon gesturing toward the screwdriver beside the dryer hinge—"thereby allowing you to see the whazzit in action. Turn on the dryer!"

"It's a trick! He's gonna kill us!"

"He'll blow the place up!"

"Squash him!"

Several Big Wigs leaped to their feet, blocking Milo's view.

Sit down! thought Milo.

"Sit down and shut up!" roared Gnash Dashman. "Or none of you is getting any boys when they come."

The Big Wigs sat.

Milo stared again at the space in the dark where the cages were. He was certain his father had cleared the row of chairs by now, but he would have to be an extraordinarily fast climber if he'd rescued the boy already. Dad was probably just now reaching the cages, Milo told himself.

"And now for the whazzit!" proclaimed Lyndon.

Milo heard a *clunk*.

"Not that way. Turn it around. No, around the . . . the other way. There you go . . . and *voilà!*"

The whazzit was in place now.

"Now," continued Lyndon, "retrieve the wet clothing from the washers."

Milo heard Gnash Dashman's voice chime in. "You'll notice that the SuperDry 2000 can handle ten—count them—ten washers full of clothing!"

"Except they're still washing!" someone yelled. "The cycle ain't done."

"Oh . . . um . . ." said Lyndon. "Well . . . while we wait, I can explain the manufacturing process. Right now, the whazzit in this demo dryer is the only one in existence, but after today, I'll be working with the Home Office so that each of you will—"

"BORING!"

"GET ON WITH IT!"

"SQUASH HIM!"

"No!" cried Lyndon. "Wait! We have dancing girls!"

"SQUASH HIM! SQUASH HIM!" shouted the Big Wigs.

"Wait! Wait! You want your Squashing? You can have your Squashing right now! We have Tuckerman!" shouted Lyndon. "See?"

Tuck gasped.

The spot in the darkness at which Milo had been staring was engulfed in a circle of brilliant light. There, indeed, was the frightened boy they were calling Tuckerman.

And there, too, clinging to the open door of the cage, was Milo's father.

26

Now's My Chance

Now's my chance, thought Milo. And this time it was.

It was his chance to help. The chance that he and his father had agreed upon. He and Tuck would set Lochinvar and Gilgamesh loose to create a diversion. But even as Milo thought it, he knew their plan would not work. The ogres would hardly notice two scrambling turkeys amid the rumbling washing machines, the tumbling dryer, and the sight of yet another Squashable human in the room. *If only the spotlight had hit a few seconds later,* Milo thought. His father would have already slipped inside the cage and would not have been seen.

He would not have been *seen.*

That was it!

"Tuck, I have an idea." Milo quickly explained his plan. "It's dangerous. I'd do it myself, but—"

"It's not a one-man job." Tuck leaped onto the awaiting Gilgamesh. A puff of elevator dust rose around her and she waved it away. "It's a two-kids-and-a-turkey job. Give me that fork. Let's go."

Milo tossed Tuck the fork and slipped in front of her onto the waiting turkey's back. Holding tight to the shoelace reins, he shouted his command. *"ALLEZ!"*

Instantly, Lochinvar took off, flapping and wurbling toward the crowd of Big Wigs. Gilgamesh charged straight ahead. Milo pulled the reins to the left, steering the galloping bird away from the crowd and toward the row of washers. Above the shouts of the ogres, Milo could hear Lyndon's amplified voice. "Get him!" he shouted. "He's climbing into the cage! See?"

"You won't see for long!" shouted Milo. "Ready, Tuck?"

Tuck raised her fork high as Milo steered Gilgamesh in front of the first washer. With a mighty clang, she swung the utensil sledgehammer-esque against it. Just as it had when the janitor had bumped it earlier, the washer door sprang open. Gallon after ogre gallon of hot, sudsy water poured

out onto the floor, and clouds of steam appeared like thick fog in the dark.

It worked! Milo wanted to cheer, but there was no time. *"Allez!"* he cried, and Gilgamesh galloped on toward the second machine. Again Tuck raised her fork, and again she brought it down hard. The second washer door popped open, and once again hot water gushed forth and steam billowed.

All around them, Milo could hear ogre voices.

"My shoes is all wet!"

"What's going on? I can't see nothing!"

Gilgamesh charged toward the third washer. It was getting more difficult to ride now as the bird slipped and slid through the soapsuds, but Milo held tight. *Smack!* The third washer opened. *Whack! Crack!* The fourth and the fifth.

"Where'd he go?" hollered someone.

"Get off me, ya big oaf!"

"Turn on the lights!"

The lights snapped on, and Milo took a quick glimpse at the room. Big Wigs were slipping and sliding, colliding with chairs and crashing into one another.

And, just as Milo had hoped, every pair of ogre glasses was completely fogged over, like the janitor's had been earlier that day. The ogres could not see a thing.

Now *that* was a diversion.

He turned his focus back to the washers just as Gilgamesh collided with the sixth one. The door flew open, nearly knocking Tuck from her seat. Instinctively, Milo grabbed hold of her arm with his free hand.

"Eyes on the road, Junior Speck," said Tuck.

Wurble-wurble, said Gilgmesh.

"Right. Sorry, buddy. Keep going. *Allez!*"

Gilgamesh regained his stride. *Smack!* The seventh washer opened. *Whack!* The eighth did not. Nor did the ninth. Tuck's arms had to be tired, but there was only one machine left. "You okay?" Milo called over his shoulder.

"Keep going!" yelled Tuck. With what Milo knew must be her last bit of strength, Tuck raised the hors d'oeuvre fork high above her head and brought it down against the tenth washer. *Crack!* The door flew from its hinges and crashed to the floor.

Wurble! Gilgamesh flapped his wings and rose into the air, landing on the top of the doorless machine.

The room was in chaos. Steam clouded the air, but Milo

could still make out the figures of battling ogres. Fists flew. Wigs flew. Then Milo saw a flash of light.

Inside the cage to which his father had been clinging just a minute ago shone the silvery zipper. Milo saw his father peer through the steamy mist toward the coils of cable where he had last seen his son. He must have thought Milo had followed the original plan, that he had set loose the turkeys and zipped away.

He watched as Dad opened the zipper. The space around it rippled as he and the frightened boy he had gone to rescue stepped through the opening. A moment later, the zipper disappeared.

"NOOOOO!"

A horrible shriek pierced the room. It was Lyndon. Despite the fact that the camera ogre had left her post to engage in a wrestling match with two Big Wigs and a chorus girl, the camera had remained pointed at the lectern and the small man who now stood cursing upon it. His face was red with anger, and a deep hatred filled his eyes. He smoothed his hair and scanned the room of battling ogres, until finally his gaze came to rest on something. Or, more accurately, someone.

Milo and Tuck had been spotted.

"Just kids," said Lyndon. He had not moved from the

microphone, and his words echoed throughout the room. "My entire plan ruined by two stupid kids." He looked hard at Tuck. "I should have fed you to a security ogre when we first got here, spoiled little thing. I suppose it's not too late." Lyndon snapped his fingers. "Suppertime, boys!"

Tuck shoved Milo's shoulder. "Go!" she yelled. "We've got to—"

"SUPPERTIME?" A freshly de-wigged ogre rose up behind the lectern. "I can't see you, but I can smell you!" he roared, raising his fists high in the air.

"Wait!" shouted Lyndon. "Not me. I meant—"

Crack! The ogre's enormous fists came down hard. The

lectern splintered, shards of wood and wires flying in all directions. The microphone squealed and thudded to the ground, perfectly placed to amplify the sickening smack of Prometheus Lyndon landing hard beside it.

27

All That Can Be Done

The ogre pawed through the rubble until he found his prey. "Come with me, Dr. Lunch!" he said, scooping up Lyndon's limp body. He sniffed, then backed cautiously away from the demolished lectern and ducked behind the silver screen, all the while muttering things like "mine, all mine" and "ranch dressing."

Milo felt Tuck shudder behind him. "You know he was going to feed us to the ogres, right?" he said

"I know," said Tuck. "But I still wish we could have captured him instead. Maybe brought him back to the Agency and made him stand trial instead of . . ."

Milo twisted around to look Tuck in the eye. "We did what could be done." Dad and that boy were safe. Jane and Ernesto and Little Dude were safe. Now all Milo had to do was say the oath, and he and Tuck would be safe too. "Everyone is safe now."

"Unless," said Tuck, pointing to the SuperDry 2000, "that thing actually works."

Tuck was right. The SuperDry 2000 was still roaring away on the stage, its door propped open, the gleaming whazzit tucked neatly in place. How long before the ogres stopped hitting each other with folding chairs and realized they could put the dryer to use? They might capture dozens, maybe hundreds, of kids before any agents arrived.

Milo looked around the room. The ogres were still battling. Most had lost their glasses as well as their wigs. All he and Tuck needed to do was fly Gilgamesh to the dryer and pop the whazzit out of its spot. How hard could that be? "As soon as I reach that boy, you'll call the zipper and go home," his father had said. And Milo had promised they would.

Well. They were going. They were just grabbing the whazzit on the way.

"You've got a plan, don't you?" said Tuck.

With a flick of the shoelace, they were off, Gilgamesh gliding from the top of the washer to a spot in front of the SuperDry

2000. The machine was even bigger than it appeared on the screen, and it roared like a jet engine. A strong wind pulled at Milo's clothes.

The dryer sat on a marble pedestal that was nearly as tall as Gilgamesh. From their seat upon the turkey, Milo and Tuck were just tall enough to see the edge of the whazzit. It would not be easy to reach. They eased closer to the dryer opening. "Steady, buddy." Milo kicked off his slippers. "Easy, now." Slowly, one bare foot at a time, he stood up on the turkey's broad back. "Fork," he said. Tuck handed him the fork, then held tight to his legs to keep him from falling. Milo hefted the utensil over his head, pushed the tines into the narrow seam between the whazzit and the dryer wall, and pulled down with all his might.

The whazzit did not budge.

"Let go of my legs." Milo lifted his feet, hoping his full weight would help pry the whazzit loose. Nothing. The hinges at the base of the gadget were doing their job. The whazzit would do what it was designed to do. The dryer would not explode. Children would be caught.

"Figures," said Milo, dropping back onto Gilgamesh. A cloud of dust and mulch rose from the bird's feathers and tickled his nose. Milo sneezed.

And then it came to him.

He looked over his shoulder. The ogre battle actually seemed to have intensified. Milo tossed Tuck the shoelace reins. "Keep Gilgamesh steady, okay?"

"What are you going to do?"

"There's no time to explain. Trust me."

An uneasy look flickered on Tuck's face.

"I'm not like Lyndon, okay?" said Milo. "We're in this together."

Tuck straightened the Excellence medal on his chest. "Stop being mushy, Speck. Get on with it."

Milo stood again. He pulled himself up onto the still-stuck fork and shimmied over to the dryer wall. The dryer roared. Hot air sucked at his hair and his clothes, threatening to pull him inside, but he held tight to the fork until he found what he was looking for.

There it was. The lint trap. Other than its enormous size, it was exactly like the one in his dryer at home, with a long plastic edge for lifting the screen out of its slot and removing whatever dust and debris had collected as the dryer did its work. Milo grabbed hold of the plastic edge, pulled himself across the whazzit, then stepped over the lint screen, turning so that his back was to the dryer drum, his toes clinging to the tiny ledge between it and the lint trap. Now he could look out at the room of battling ogres, but he tried not to. Instead, he kept his eyes on Tuck and the wind-ruffled feathers of Gilgamesh.

With a great heave, he lifted the screen, drawing it up as high as he could reach. A good ogre inch remained in the slot. Milo stood tall and held tight, looking through the screen at Tuck.

"Dance with me!" he shouted over the roar of the dryer.

"What?"

"Dance!" hollered Milo. He began to sing as loud as he could. *"First you flap and then you flap, then you wiggle and you wiggle, then stomp your feet."* Tuck joined in. *"First you flap and then you flap, then you wiggle and you wiggle, then stomp your feet.* C'mon, Gilgamesh! Dance!"

Gilgamesh danced. With every flap and wiggle, clouds of dust and bits of dried leaf rose from the turkey's feathers and were sucked straight toward the dryer, catching in the lint trap that Milo held up before him.

"Then you flap and then you flap, and you wiggle and you wiggle," Milo sang as clumps of carpet fiber and turkey down filled the screen. All he had to do was hold on. Once the trap was completely filled, he would jam it back down into place and—if he was right—he could shake the debris loose and clog the tiny vent behind it.

If they were lucky, the lint would catch fire and the dryer would explode, destroying itself and the whazzit.

"Then stomp your feet!" Milo sang. The screen was almost completely covered now, and Tuck and Gilgamesh were obscured from view. It was time. Milo shoved the screen deep into its slot, then shook it up and down as hard as he could to loosen all that had been trapped. Each time he raised the screen, less lint clung to it. He could almost picture the vent filling with turkey down and mulch, and it felt as if the air around him was growing hotter.

"It's working!" he hollered to Tuck. "I'm coming back out now!" He looked through the screen to give her a triumphant smile   only to find his grin matched by that of Roger,

the singing security ogre. Roger had Gilgamesh by the neck. In his other hand was the Head of the Tuckerman Agency.

"Tuck!" yelled Milo.

"You got me in a lot of trouble, Tuckerman. But you ain't gonna get away this time. Wait till I show my boss what I caught!" With a laugh, he hurled both girl and bird into the dryer.

Wurble-wurble, warned Gilgamesh, as he, Tuck, and Milo collided. Milo lost hold of the lint screen and tumbled into the roaring dryer drum, thumping again and again against its hard metal walls.

"Don't go anywhere. I'll be right back!" The security ogre pulled the screwdriver from the hinge and slammed the dryer door, leaving Milo, Tuck, and Gilgamesh spinning and thudding in the dark.

"Call the zipper!" yelled Tuck.

Desperately, Milo tried to remember the oath. "I swear as a Tuckerman Agent . . ." he began. A bright red light flashed inside the dryer. Milo heard a crackle and a hiss. He smelled smoke and burning feathers. The light flashed again.

"No!" hollered Milo as he banged hard against the dryer barrel. His head swam, and then . . .

Boom!

28

Heaven

For a long time, Milo had the sensation of spinning. And then falling. And then, somehow, rising. *Am I dead?* he wondered. *Am I going to heaven?*

A sudden bright light nearly blinded him. Milo felt something poke his leg.

"What are you doing in there?" said a voice he knew very well. It was not the voice of an angel. It was the voice of Grandmother.

Milo blinked and looked around. He was not in heaven. He was folded—origami-esque—inside the uncomfortably cramped drum of his basement clothes dryer.

In the books that Milo read, it was sometimes the case that the hero bumped his head and was transported to another world where he had some dramatic adventure, only to wake up in a hospital or in his own bed and discover that his entire experience had been nothing more than a dream. He had always felt cheated at the end of such books and could not help feeling that way now.

"Figures," he said as he climbed out of the dryer.

"'Figures' is right." Grandmother slammed the dryer door. "What's that all over those pants? How did you shrink that new shirt?"

Milo held out an arm. His ducky shirt *had* shrunk. The sleeves were a good three inches shorter than they had been this morning. His pants were shorter too.

"Go upstairs and change," ordered Grandmother just as a metallic knock echoed inside the dryer.

"Excuse me," said a voice.

Grandmother screamed, and Milo flung open the dryer door. "Tuck!" he cried. It had not been a dream. It had not been a dream at all! "Are you okay?"

"Fine," she said, crawling out of the dryer barrel. "Hey, Junior Speck, you don't look so junior anymore. Good thing, too. I was worried you wouldn't meet the height requirement for some of the training centers."

"Training centers?"

"If you're going to be a Tuckerman Agent, you're going to need proper training," said Tuck. "We all do."

Wurble-wurble. Grandmother screamed again as Gilgamesh appeared. Unlike Milo, who seemed to have grown during his dryer transport, the bird had shrunk quite noticeably. He was now no bigger than a parrot.

"What is that?!" Grandmother's eyes were wide and she hopped from one foot to the other, like a cartoon lady who had just seen a mouse.

"He's a turkey. His name is Gilgamesh," said Milo.

"If you think for one second that I'm going to be responsible for another—"

A loud ring shocked her into screaming once more. This time the sound did not come from inside the clothes dryer, but from the pocket of Grandmother's housecoat. "Oh, my nerves," she muttered, pulling out a shiny metal device.

"Hey," said Milo. "That's a ZoomBaby!"

"It's a nuisance," Grandmother grumbled. "Your father makes me carry it around, but if I turn it on, it buzzes and beeps at me. Off, stupid thing. OFF!" She poked the screen so violently, Milo was certain it would shatter.

"Let me," he said, quickly taking the glowing device from her massive hands. On the screen was the now-familiar Tracker grid. In the center was the equally familiar red dot that Milo knew indicated the location of the ZoomBaby he held. HOME it said above the dot.

Tuck looked over his shoulder. "We've finally got a signal, so we can see who's who." She tapped a blue dot that hovered a few centimeters from the first. The dot, as it turned out, was not actually one dot, but many, and as Tuck zoomed in, Milo could see at least fifty names scroll across the screen, though only one of them mattered to him.

"There!" cried Milo. "Right there! Samson Speck! Where is he, Tuck? Where's my dad?"

Tuck tapped the ZoomBaby again, and four words appeared on the screen:

GUINEVERE'S
PIZZA AND SUBS.

29

No Shoes, No Service

It took Milo and Tuck several minutes to convince Grand-mother that the now-diminutive Gilgamesh would not attack her while they were gone, and several more minutes were spent in Milo's fruitless quest for footwear. His slippers were back in Ogregon, and, thanks to his dryer-travel growth spurt, his feet no longer fit into any of his Barely Boys shoes, but he was not ready to fill his father's shoes yet either. In the end, despite the Thanksgiving Day snow that had just begun to fall, he had no choice but to go without, and so it was that when he and Tuck burst into the warm, tomato-scented lobby of his favorite pizza place, Milo did so barefoot.

Dad didn't even notice.

"Milo!" he cried, sweeping his son into his arms. "You're safe! You're both safe!" A great deal of laughing and swing-ing and squeezing ensued before Milo's feet touched the cool

tile floor again. "Let me look at you, son. Is it possible that you've grown?"

"I think I stretched in the dryer," said Milo.

"And Tuck!" Dad looked as if he wanted to hug her, too, but instead he extended a hand, which Tuck shook with enthusiasm. "You're safe. When I zipped back home and you two weren't here, I was afraid something terrible had happened. The Tuckerman rescue team was already on its way to Ogregon and I wanted to go with them, but nobody would take me, since I had been fired."

Tuck winced. "I'm sorry. I'll get you reinstated as soon as I can. I swear."

Dad waved her worries away. "It wasn't your fault. I know that. Everyone knows that now. Someone logged me into a ZoomBaby so I could watch the team's progress, but the network still isn't working in Ogregon. I had to wait for someone to zip back with news. They reached Ogregon just in time to witness your heroism, but before they could reach you . . . they thought you had been caught in the explosion. They thought . . ." Dad's voice cracked. "But then Grandmother called about a vicious attack-chicken prowling the basement and eventually got around to mentioning that you and Tuck were on your way here. What happened? I want to hear everything. Wait—" Dad hugged Milo again, then hurried to the dining room doorway to flag the hostess. "Guinevere? Can we get a booth?"

A plump woman with wiry red hair and a regal air appeared. "I'd be happy to seat you, but I don't believe a booth will be large enough," she said as Jane, Ernesto, and Little Dude raced into the lobby behind her.

"*¡Patito!*" A small, round-faced boy rushed to Milo's side and hugged his legs.

"Little Dude!" said Milo.

"Glad to see you, guys," said Jane. "What happened? You okay? Did you catch that bad guy?"

"An angry ogre took care of that for us," said Tuck. The smile that had been growing on her face was gone. Lyndon had betrayed her. He had let her father die and had been ready to have her killed, too. And yet, Milo realized, it must have been awful to see the man who had been a father figure to her Squashed like that.

"Less talking, more eating," interrupted Guinevere. "I'm going to put you in the party room, since this seems like a celebration. Plus"—she looked at Tuck—"it will give you a little privacy. Samson, why don't you lead the way?"

As they all turned to follow Dad to the party room, Milo

felt a hand on his shoulder. "Just a minute, young man," said the regal hostess. She plucked a piece of moldy sandwich from his ducky shirt. "I won't have you parading through my dining room looking—and smelling—like this." She looked at Milo's feet and then over at the NO SHOES, NO SERVICE sign.

"But, I just—"

"Rules are rules." Guinevere strode to a door marked EMPLOYEES ONLY and waved Milo toward it. "Come along. I've got some spare uniforms in here."

Milo had seen the Guinevere's Pizza and Subs uniforms before. With the exception of Guinevere, every employee in the place wore a brightly colored jester's outfit, complete with curly-toed shoes and a sproingy hat adorned with bells. Milo had felt sorry for them every time he and his dad had come in for a slice.

"I don't—" started Milo, but then Guinevere looked at the NO SHOES sign again.

Fine. He had been wearing a googly-eyed ducky shirt all day. How much worse could a jester's outfit be?

Guinevere pulled open the Employees Only door. Behind it lay a large wood-paneled room. A painting of a knight with a needle sword and a button shield hung on the wall.

A nearby desk was covered with snack-food wrappers. Milo recognized the place instantly.

"Holy smokes! Tuckerman Headquarters is part of Guinevere's Pizza and Subs?"

Guinevere laughed. "Guinevere's is part of Tuckerman Agency Headquarters. This is just a spare Agency office we use for transport and storage. The real nexus of the place is a floor beneath us." She tapped a wall panel, which slid away to reveal a tidy closet filled with crisp navy suits, pristine white shirts, and neat rows of shiny brown shoes.

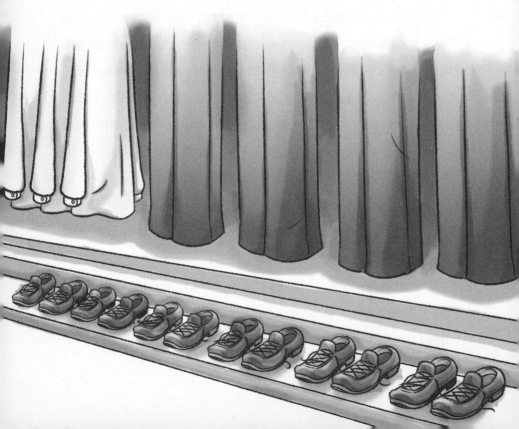

"Tuckerman Agency uniforms!" said Milo. He almost laughed.

"What did you think? You and Ms. Tuck would return from destroying that whizz-bang thing—"

"Whazzit," said Milo.

"Yes, whazzit—and I'd welcome you home by dressing you up like one of my busboys?"

"I wasn't sure . . ." said Milo, though in truth, he was no longer thinking about uniforms. "The whazzit was destroyed? Are you sure?"

"One hundred percent sure. Every ogre in the place ran away screaming after you blew up that dryer. Our rescue agents rushed in to see if they could find you and Ms. Tuck. They didn't, of course, but they did find the pieces of the whazzit—all beyond repair."

They had done it. Their plan had worked. He and Tuck had destroyed the whazzit.

Guinevere had turned her attention back to the closet. "Stand here," she said, steering Milo toward a mirror. She draped a Tuckerman Agency jacket over his shoulders to check the size.

"There you are," she said.

And there he was.

Milo Speck, Tuckerman Agent.

Barefoot. A purple bruise on his forehead. A googly-eyed ducky on his chest. But taller. Stronger-looking than he had been that morning. And smiling. Milo couldn't help smiling.

"I wish your mother could see you now," said Guinevere. "She'll be so proud when she hears what you've done."

Milo met Guinevere's eyes in the mirror. "You think she's alive?"

"Of course she's alive. Eleanor Speck is a top agent. A smart cookie, and wholly dedicated to her work. Nothing is going to get in the way of your mother finishing what she started—whether that is some secret independent mission, or reuniting with her family." She patted him gently on the shoulder, and Milo looked at his reflection again.

He was a Tuckerman Agent, ready to start training. Which meant that whether Dad was one or not, they could zip wherever they needed to search for Mom. Eventually, they would find her. He and Dad would do all that could be done. Together.

"I'm going to bring a new jacket to Ms. Tuck and leave you to get dressed. Do you have everything? Shirt, suit, shoes . . . oh, I almost forgot!" Guinevere opened a narrow drawer and pulled out a pair of socks. They were navy blue with spots. Or dots. "Check to make sure I gave you a matching pair. I can't always tell the pink from the yellow."

Milo checked.

"They're perfect," he said.

30

The Beginning

The party room at Guinevere's Pizza and Subs was often rented out for children's birthdays and was usually filled with games and balloons and colorful banners celebrating the guest of honor. When Milo arrived, his old clothes tucked under his arm, he half anticipated seeing a candlelit cake on the round center table. There was no cake, but even if there had been, Milo would not have been able to see it, for the room was so crowded with Tuckerman Agents that all he could see were dozens of besuited backs. He could, however, hear Tuck.

"There's no way the ogres can develop a new whazzit now that Lyndon's . . ."

"Gone," Milo heard Dad finish.

"Right. Now that Lyndon is gone," said Tuck. "All the

same, we need to make sure every dryer in Ogregon is destroyed and that they can't make any more."

An older agent standing in front of a pin-the-tail-on-the-donkey poster scowled. "Felix Tuckerman—your father, Agent Tuck—would launch an attack. He'd fight!"

"And my great-grandfather, Amos Tuckerman, would not," replied Tuck. "We're going to negotiate. Ogregon will agree to use clotheslines, and we will agree to send in our best agricultural agents to give them another shot at raising beef and pork."

Milo heard one or two agents grumble, but most supported Tuck's plan.

"Tuck's exactly right," said another agent. She was wearing a sparkly purple birthday hat, but spoke with great seriousness. "That is exactly what Amos would have done."

"Amos also would have known that returning heroes need to eat." Guinevere had stepped into the party room behind Milo, followed by several jester-waiters bearing the most delicious-looking pizza he had ever seen. "And we don't want these children's parents to get here and find them half-starved either, do we? Go on, get back to work. Scat!"

Reluctantly, the agents scatted. Now Milo could see the

table and the five people seated around it: Jane, Ernesto, Little Dude. Tuck. Dad. They could see him too.

"Looking sharp, Junior Speck," said Tuck.

Guinevere patted Milo's shoulder. "You eat," she said, reaching for the old clothes he still had tucked under his arm. "And I'll take these."

Milo handed over the pants, but held on to the sweatshirt. "Actually, I was thinking that Little Dude might want this." He unpinned the Excellence medal and dropped it into his jacket pocket. "I mean, it's kind of smelly right now, but . . ." He held the sweatshirt out to the small boy, who hugged it tight to his chest.

"*Patito,*" said Little Dude.

Quank, sighed the ducky happily. *Quank, Quank, Quank.*

Few things will increase one's appetite for supper as much a day spent avoiding being someone else's, and so it was that little was spoken in the party room of Guinevere's Pizza and Subs until well after the light outside had dimmed. Finally, when everyone's bellies were full and Guinevere's offer of just one more slice had been waved away, she sat at the table with them.

"If you were here tomorrow," she said, "I would have made you a proper Thanksgiving dinner instead."

It was Thanksgiving tomorrow! Milo had forgotten! And yet here he was, a Tuckerman Agent, sitting between Tuck and Dad, feeling more truly, deeply thankful than he had in a long time.

"This was better than Thanksgiving dinner," he told Guinevere. "Besides, I don't think I'll ever want to eat turkey again."

"Thank you, Guinevere," said Tuck. "Thank all of you — Milo, Mr. Speck, Jane — for all you did today."

"It sounds like it was quite a day. You must be very tired," said Guinevere. "The children's parents will be here soon, and most of the agents have gone home for the night. Ms. Tuck, I don't know if you've already made plans, but you're welcome to stay with me for a while."

"Actually," said Tuck, "Agent Speck and his dad have made a similar offer." She looked at Milo. "I'm inclined to take them up on it, but before I do, I need to understand just how it was that Junior Speck here got to Ogregon in the first place."

"I'm still not entirely sure myself," said Milo.

"Start at the beginning," said Dad. "Maybe we can all figure it out together."

The beginning, thought Milo. Okay. But what was the beginning?

Was it when he was born to two Tuckerman Agents? When he was a little kid and Dad read him stories every night? When Mom went away? When Grandmother came and he felt so alone? Or was the beginning just today, this morning, when he was all by himself, dreaming of heroic adventures and exotic locales?

Milo's throat was scratchy from yelling dance moves over the roar of the dryer. When he spoke, his voice was deeper and quieter than he expected it would be, but no one asked him to speak up.

Instead, the room grew hushed. It was as if the very walls were leaning in to listen.

"It all started," said Milo, "with a sock."

A Note from the Author

If you enjoyed *Milo Speck, Accidental Agent* even the least little bit, you are certain to like the work of two writers who inspired it: Roald Dahl and Edward Eager. Of Mr. Dahl's many books for young readers, my favorite is either *The BFG* or *Danny, Champion of the World,* both of which are a perfect balance of humor and heart. If you haven't yet read anything by Mr. Eager, you must rectify the situation, pronto. Start with *Half Magic.* It is funny and smart and filled with adventure. After *Half Magic,* you can find your way around the rest of the magic books in whatever order you please, but don't miss *Knight's Castle,* whatever you do.

As long as there's some space left on this page, I'd like to thank some other inspirational people. Jeannette Larson — sharp of wit and editorial acumen, but never of tongue — must be thanked for her hard work and gentle guidance through the many (many) drafts of this book. A special Excellence medal goes to designer Lisa Vega for her utmost fidelity to this project. Thank you to Mariano Epelbaum for the witty, wonderful art. Thanks are also due Jack

Thompson, Kate Messner, Leda Schubert, and Ellen Miles for reading *Milo Speck* countless times and offering valuable counsel. Other folks listened patiently as I talked through plot, character arc, writing challenges, and song lyrics. These dear friends include Claire Thompson, Loree Griffin Burns, Marla Frazee, Myra Wolfe, Kelly Ramsdell Fineman, Kristy Dempsey, Sara Lewis Holmes, Anne Marie Pace, Katy Duffield, Kathy Erskine, Alma Fullerton, Cassandra Whetstone, Tanya Seale, and countless innocent people who found themselves in the wrong place at the wrong time.

Finally, I offer my deepest gratitude to Julio Thompson, for unwavering faith, encouragement, and willingness to laugh at my jokes.